SILENT ARE THE DEAD

SILENT ARE THE DEAD

GEORGE HARMON COXE

MYSTERIOUSPRESS.COM

OPEN ROAD
INTEGRATED MEDIA
NEW YORK

Copyright © 1941 by George Harmon Coxe

Cover design by Mumtaz Mustafa

ISBN 978-1-4532-3678-9

This 2013 edition published by MysteriousPress.com/ Open Road Integrated Media
345 Hudson Street
New York, NY 10014
www.mysteriouspress.com
www.openroadmedia.com

SILENT ARE THE DEAD

CHAPTER ONE

THE CAMERA EYE

FOR OVER AN HOUR the five news-photographers had been waiting in the stuffy, smoke-filled corridor, and their boredom had reached the stage of grumbling and profanity when Kline, of the *News,* peered through the glass insert in the courtroom door and gave the announcement they had been waiting for.

"Hey. This looks like it."

"And about time," somebody said sourly.

Casey, number-one camera for the *Express,* sighed with relief and stepped on his cigarette. He gave his camera a final glance and moved back just as the leather-covered doors slapped open and three leg men from the afternoon sheets barged out and headed for the telephones in the hope of making the final.

"What about it?" Kline yelled.

"He's bein' held in twenty thousand."

"Twenty thousand?" Weidler of the *Globe* made noises with his tongue. "Think of that. I guess they ain't kiddin'."

"I never thought they'd get that baby," Kline said. "He was the smartest prosecutor this town ever had."

Casey was thinking the same thing. Until he had retired to

private practice five years ago, Stanford Endicott had made a record as an Assistant Attorney that had been the talk of the East. Now—

The doors opened again and there he was, flanked by reporters, smiling, a big impressive-looking man, plain-faced, imperturbable.

"Over here, please, Mr. Endicott," they said.

Stanford Endicott kept on smiling. "Wait a minute, boys," he said, and put on his hat to cover up the wide streak of baldness down the center of his skull. "Shoot," he said.

Casey pressed the shutter release and was conscious of the bursts of light from the five flash guns; then he was backing down the hall, exchanging a fresh bulb for the used one, hearing the barrage of questions that fell from the reporters' mouths.

"Will you handle your own defense—? Can't you give us a statement? Something we can quote you on?"

"Sorry, boys." Endicott kept coming, and Casey continued his retreat until he shot the second picture. "Nothing now. You can say that I have every confidence of clearing myself of this charge, but I can make no further statement until I've seen the District Attorney."

He went by Casey, still trailing reporters from his coattails, and the big photographer went back along the corridor and picked up his plate case. By the time he had reached the sidewalk, Endicott had gone and the newspapermen had dispersed; all but Tom Wade, who stood at the curb slipping his own camera back in his plate case.

"Get anything?" Casey asked.

"Caught him coming down the steps."

Casey handed him the exposed film holder. "Take it back to the office."

"What about you?"

"I got to see a guy."

Wade, a round-faced, blue-eyed youth with an infectious grin and an incurable curiosity, looked dubious. "In a bar, I'll bet."

"Go on," said Casey. "Quit arguin'." For although his date was in a bar, it was not, as Wade would have suspected, entirely for drinking.

Kelly's Bar & Grill was about half a block from the *Express* building and Casey paused outside to fold a twenty-dollar bill down to the approximate size of an air-mail stamp. It was just five o'clock then, but there were not more than a half-dozen men at the age-darkened bar, and the one he sought stood by himself halfway down its length, a small man in a wrinkled suit and shoes run-down at the heels. Mike, the head bartender, stopped daydreaming long enough to indicate the man and say softly, "He says he's waiting for you."

"He is—Hello, Ned," Casey said, and put out his hand.

The man turned. His eyes were tired, so was his smile; then, as his hand touched Casey's and felt the folded bill, the smile was suddenly grateful and an awkwardness came upon him as he tried to speak.

"Rye," Casey said to Mike, who had followed behind the bar. "Ned?"

The man looked at his empty glass and shook his head. "No, thanks, Flash," he said. "I got to be running. You'll get it back, all of it," he said when Mike was out of hearing. "I think it'll be a week from Monday."

"Stick with it, kid," Casey said, and watched the man move toward the door. He was still following him with his somber gaze when Mike shoved the bottle at him and slid a chaser along the mahogany.

"You'll never get it back," he said.

Casey looked at him. He poured a drink and pushed back his hat. He looked at Mike again disgustedly. "You know everything, Mike. All bartenders know everything."

"He's been living off'n you for a month."

"And now he's got a job on the *News*. He's going to work a week from Monday." He tipped his head and let the rye slide down his throat. He reached for the water glass and turned it in his big hand. "It must be nice to know everything."

Mike got red in the face and his eyes were ashamed. He filled Casey's glass again, a signal that this one was on the house, and went away. Someone came in but Casey was not aware of this until a man stopped beside him and ordered bourbon. It was Vaughn, who covered the State House for the *Express*.

"You down on that Endicott thing?" he said. "What happened?" Casey told him.

Vaughn drank. "Twenty thousand bail, huh? Funny. I'll bet he put more guys away than any Assistant D.A. we had and now he's getting it himself—for receiving stolen property."

"You think he's got a chance?"

"No. His best bet would be to make a deal and take a plea," Vaughn said. "And he probably knows it. This thing has been going on for quite a while. A gang knocks off a bank or mortgage company and gets away with some bonds—this time it was some outfit in New Haven. Remember? About a month ago? Two hundred thousand in bonds? Well, the insurance company gets word the bonds can be had— for maybe fifteen or twenty percent. Instead of taking a chance of having to pay out two hundred grand, they lay out maybe thirty thousand and get back the bonds and no questions asked. Which is okay with the mob because they don't have to worry about peddling them hot or forging the serial numbers. It's good, clean dough to them."

"And Endicott was the contact man," Casey said.

"Sure. And now the insurance company is going to be in a spot too. The Feds have been working on this thing. They're going to ask a lot of questions. When they walked in on him, there he was with the bonds on the desk and the insurance representative ready to pay out. Remember Noel Scaffa, the private dick in New York who used to do the same thing on jewel robberies? Well, he wound up in the can. So will Endicott."

The phone rang while Vaughn was talking, and Mike yelled to Casey.

"Who is it?" Casey asked. "What's he want?"

Mike grinned. "He says to tell that no-good so-and-so to get on here and be quick about it."

"Sounds like Blaine," Vaughn said, referring to the city editor.

"Yeah," said Casey. "He's my pal."

It was Blaine, all right, and his voice was curt and sarcastic. "Where are those shots of Stanford Endicott?"

"Wade's got 'em."

"And where's Wade?"

"Well, he's—" Casey broke off. "Ain't he there?"

"No. And for your information there's a riot up on the Common. You know the Common? I hate to annoy you with such trifles, but I thought it might be nice if the *Express* could have a picture of it, don't you? No hurry, of course. It'll probably wait for you."

Casey tossed coins on the bar and swept up his plate case. "Some day, so help me," he said, "I'm going to hit him right in the nose."

He could see the crowd up the street as he went out on the sidewalk. That made him forget Blaine and he started to run. He was only a block from Tremont and when he reached it he saw the patrol wagon and squad cars at the opposite curb.

Over by the bandstand the police were dispersing what remained of the rioters. A few of them were fleeing down the slope toward

Charles, but it was apparent that most of the action was over. Casey got out his camera and screwed in a flash bulb as a burly, uniformed cop came through the fringe of the crowd with an arm lock on a skinny, disheveled-looking fellow without a hat. The cop had a cut on his lip and looked grim; the prisoner had a handkerchief clamped across a bloody nose.

Casey got a picture and reversed his film holder. As he put in a new flash bulb two more cops came along with a battered-looking individual between them. Casey put up the camera and then, with his finger on the shutter release, he stopped, lowered the camera, and gaped, jaw sagging.

The round-faced, forlorn-looking specimen getting the police escort had his hat jammed on his head. His face was dirty, there was a lump on his cheekbone. One coat pocket had been ripped, and a torn necktie fluttered under one ear. He wasn't resisting, but he was arguing loudly and holding on to something he carried protectively under his coat. This something was a camera and the voice was Tom Wade's.

"Where you goin' with him?" Casey demanded.

"Where do you think, bud?" the cop said. "Take a walk," said the other, not looking around. "On your way before we give you a ride."

"For free, Mulloy?"

The cop stopped and gave him the eye. Then his red face relaxed in a grin. "Oh, Flash Gun. Kinda late, ain't yuh?"

"What'd he do?" Casey indicated Wade.

"We don't know. He was just in the middle. He gave us an argument."

Hope came at last to Tom Wade and his voice was relieved. "Tell these apes to lay off, Flash."

"Who's an ape?" Mulloy demanded.

"Don't mind him," Casey said. "He's punch-drunk. Here, I'll take him," he said, and stepped between Wade and Mulloy.

"You mean he works with you?" Mulloy said.

"Certainly. And there'll be plenty of grief for him when he gets back without you guys making it tougher."

"Well—" Mulloy was doubtful.

"You don't want the *Express* down on you, do you?" Casey said, and went off with Wade, leaving the two policemen standing there.

Wade pulled his camera out from under his coat. It looked all right to Casey, but he noticed there was no film holder in it; then, before he could speak, Wade cursed, wheeled abruptly, and sprinted back through the thinning crowd. Near the bandstand he checked his pace, glanced about, and with Casey trailing as best he could, ran to a bench a short distance away.

Here, Wade's plate case between them, sat two smutty-faced urchins. One was pulling slides out of film holders and making a neat pile of them, the other was juggling flash bulbs. Wade yelled and bore down on them and they jumped up. One of them threw a flash bulb at him and legged it across the grass; his companion followed, the plate case in one hand. When he saw Wade was gaining, he dropped the case.

Casey sat down on the bench and blew out his breath. He looked down at the pile of film holders and slides, knowing now that every last film had been exposed to light and ruined. Wade trudged up with the plate case, moaned when he saw the condition of the film holders, and sank disconsolately down beside Casey, who let a full minute drag by before he spoke.

"You didn't go to the office, huh?"

"I was just goin' in when I heard the commotion. I beat it up here. It was just gettin' good. Guys slugging each other all over the place."

"What about?"

"I don't know. It was just a free-for-all when I got there. I got one good shot and was taking another when some guy saw me and yelled."

"So?"

"They all stopped slugging and jumped on me."

"Those shots of Endicott are here, huh?" Casey picked up the film holders, sighed, and tossed them in the case. "Blaine will love this," he said wearily, "and don't think he won't say so."

CHAPTER TWO

HEADING FOR TROUBLE

BLAINE, THE CITY EDITOR, leaned back in his chair and listened to the story Casey told. He was a slender, prematurely gray man with a sharp, angular face and cold gray eyes. Admittedly the best desk man in the city, he was a curt, unsociable fellow, who dressed immaculately and seldom raised his voice, depending instead on barbed words which he thrust home sarcastically and twisted expertly.

"Very interesting," he said. "Two of you out all afternoon and I get this." He touched the print Casey had offered—the one of the cop and the rioter—with a pencil in a gesture of distaste.

Casey set his jaw and said nothing. Long experience had shown him that there was no percentage in trying to battle Blaine with words, so he just waited there in front of the desk, a rugged, thick-chested man who stood better than six foot one and weighed 215 pounds, none of it fat. His brown hair was peppered with gray at the sides and shaggy at the nape. His face was broad and homely, though distinctive because of the strength and vitality it reflected, and he kept his stare deliberate and morose as he waited for Blaine to continue.

"Nothing on Stanford Endicott, of course. That would be too much to expect." Blaine sat up. "Unfortunately, I'm afraid our competitors will all carry pictures of Mr. Endicott in the morning. Don't you think we should have one too? If it's not too much trouble? Now? Today?"

Blaine hesitated, though he knew there would be no answer. He cocked an eye at Wade, who had cleaned up and now looked fairly presentable. "I won't bother you about it," he continued. "I've got another assignment for you." He glanced at a slip of paper on his desk. "The West Roxbury Little Theater Group is putting on a play tonight. That should be right up your alley."

Wade opened his mouth, closed it with an effort. Blaine turned to Casey. "I still want a picture of Endicott," he said. "Sometime before morning, if you don't mind— If you don't think you can handle it, I'll send Austin and O'Hearn with you."

At the elevators they split, Wade deciding to go out for his dinner and Casey continuing down the stairs to the studio. He was still muttering when he entered, and he was so intent on his corrosive thoughts of Blaine that he reached the center of the room before he saw the girl.

She was sitting on a battered straight-backed chair along one wall, her feet flat on the floor, her hands in her lap, and a look of determination on her young face. She wore a loose-fitting suit of brown tweed and a felt hat cocked pertly on one side, and Casey got a quick impression of feminine attractiveness before he had a chance to notice all the details which contributed to the picture.

"Oh, hello," he said for the want of something better, good-looking young women being as scarce in the studio as pearls in restaurant oysters. "Looking for someone?"

"How do you do," she said. "Does a Mr. Austin work here?"

"Perry Austin? Yes."

"You—you're not—"

"Un-uh," Casey said. "He isn't in."

"Oh." He took her moment of indecision to note the fine-boned face, the hazel eyes, the chestnut hair with auburn lights in it; he saw too that her mouth was still somewhat tight and determined, and he decided she would be a lot prettier if only she would smile. "You don't know when he'll be back?" she added finally.

Casey said he didn't. It might be any time, and was there anything he could do?

"I'm afraid not." She rose, smoothing out her suit, and her mouth relaxed a little. "Thank you just the same."

He watched her move to the door, suggesting tentatively, "You wouldn't want to leave your name?"

"I don't believe so," she said. "Perhaps I can see him later."

It was after 8:00 when Casey got back to the studio. His earlier attempts to get in touch with Endicott had failed, so he had declared a truce while he went down the street and put away three old-fashioneds and a steak. Now, coming through the doorway to resume his pursuit of the lawyer, he saw Perry Austin sitting at his desk manicuring his fingernails. Casey sat down and reached for the telephone.

"There was a dame looking for you," he said.

Austin glanced up. "What kind of a dame?"

"How do I know? I don't run around with dames—much."

"Well, what did she look like?"

"Offhand," Casey said, grinning, "I'd say she looked a little too good for you." And he went on to describe the girl as best he could.

Austin could not seem to identify her. "Damned if I know who she is," he said, frowning. "Funny she didn't want to leave her name— She didn't say what she wanted?"

Casey answered absently as he got busy on the telephone again, and after a few minutes he located Stanford Endicott, the houseboy at his apartment informing him that the lawyer had gone to his office.

"I thought you covered him this afternoon," Austin said as the big photographer hung up.

"I did," Casey said, and, in no mood to explain, added, "I have to get some more."

Austin went back to his fingernails and Casey studied him a moment before reaching for his plate case. A symmetrically slender and regular-featured fellow in his late twenties, Austin had been dubbed the fashion plate of the *Express* because of his liking for society and night-club assignments and his penchant for sartorial splendor. He had come from somewhere in the West two years ago, and although Casey had never been particularly friendly with him, he recognized him as a competent man with a camera in spite of the wave in his hair and the small clipped mustache that did not entirely hide the suggestion of weakness about the mouth. Right now he was especially resplendent in a double-breasted dinner jacket, and as he lounged behind his desk he seemed out of place in the studio.

"What're you on?" Casey asked.

"I'm going down to the Club Berkely. They're having the finals in that 'Most Popular Model Contest.'"

"How's chances for a lift?"

"Now?"

Austin put away his nail file and shrugged. "All right," he said finally. "I'm a little early but—"

Casey put some extra flash bulbs and fresh film holders in his case, slipped into his balmacaan. He watched Austin shift the red carnation from the dinner jacket to the buttonhole of his Chesterfield.

"Sometimes," he said dryly, "I wonder if you aren't wasting your time."

"How?" Austin frowned.

"Instead of takin' pictures maybe you ought to pose for 'em."

"Just because a fellow's a photographer—" Austin began.

"Is no sign he can't be smartly dressed," Casey finished. "You told me that before— Well, let's get started."

The building where Stanford Endicott had his offices was a small but neatly modern structure in beige brick and limestone, one of the growing row that had forced the neighboring ancient red-brick fronts to masquerade with false façades in a desperate attempt to recapture some semblance of smartness.

Austin parked his coupé beyond the entrance and as Casey was opening the door, he saw the man come through the arched doorway. The light from the foyer was behind him and Casey did not see the face until the fellow passed the window of a dress shop next door. By that time Casey was on the sidewalk, and as he stood there the man glanced over his shoulder. For just an instant their eyes met; then the fellow had disappeared in the shadows and Casey knew who he was: Nat Garrison, a onetime welterweight who had been sent to Charlestown some years previous for assault with a dangerous weapon.

So he's out, Casey thought, and as Austin came round the car, he tried to think back, to recall whether Endicott had been the lawyer who defended Garrison, or whether Endicott had at that time been the prosecutor.

"I might as well go up as wait out here," Austin said.

Casey said he might as well and they went along the foyer to the single automatic elevator. "Of course we're liable to get thrown out," he added. "I haven't got an appointment, you know."

"I'd rather get thrown out with you than anybody I know," Austin said, and pushed the button marked 3. "Remember that Bund meeting?"

"Yeah," Casey said, and thinking about it helped to re-establish Austin in his estimation. The guy was a smoothy and went for the night life and soft assignments, but when the chips were down he could handle himself. They'd both got their lumps at that Bund meeting, but they were battling back to back at the finish. "We had fun that day, huh?"

There were six doors opening on the third-floor hall and the three that made up the left-hand side were given over to Stanford Endicott, the rear two being of plain wood and the first bearing a frosted-glass panel which said, *Stanford Endicott—Enter Here.*

Casey found this door unlocked. He opened it and went in. There was no direct light here, but he saw it was a large room and sufficient illumination came through the glass panel of the connecting door to make the layout discernible. There was a railed-in space to make a waiting-room of sorts, a settee, and some chairs; the balance of the floor was given over to desks and chairs and typewriters and filing cabinets.

Austin shut the door. Casey pushed past the gate ill the rail, crossed to the glass-paneled door and opened it. He took one more step; then stopped short, still holding to the knob, feeling Austin bump against his back, but not moving.

This room was smaller than the first, but not small. There were two room-high windows at one side, a leather divan, two leather chairs to match, a massive and expensive-looking desk in one corner, behind which was a high-backed chair that probably cost as much as the desk. The pile in the over-all, sand-colored rug was long enough to trip over, and almost in the center of it was Stanford Endicott.

He was on his back, one arm outflung, his knees straight and ankles crossed, as though he had done it on purpose. Casey didn't think he had; Casey thought he was dead.

Behind him Perry Austin made a quick, sucking sound and began to curse with a curious, hushed intensity that seemed, in all that stillness, shockingly loud. When he tried to crowd past, Casey moved out of the way, stepping quickly to the lawyer's side, seeing then the slowly widening puddle of blood inching from under the back of the coat. He dropped to one knee and picked up a limp wrist.

It was warm, as warm as life itself. But there was no pulse. He didn't put his hand inside the vest to feel for a heart beat because just about where the heart should be were two tiny frayed holes in the gray fabric. Austin spoke softly behind him.

"Dead?"

"Very dead," said Casey, his face somber.

CHAPTER THREE

CLOSE-UP OF A CORPSE

FOR A LONG MINUTE Casey and Austin stared silently at the inert figure. The long, plain-looking face was heavy in death, and Casey found himself thinking about how Endicott had looked that afternoon coming out of the courtroom. He could, in imagination, see the smiling, confident face again, hear the booming voice. He found himself looking at the bald streak which was no longer pink, but white and shiny and naked.

"You're going to get a picture all right," Austin said. "But not the one Blaine figured on."

"Yeah." Casey opened the camera and reached for a flash bulb.

"He hasn't been dead long either."

"Minutes. He's still warm." And as Casey screwed the flash bulb in the synchronized holder he thought again of Nat Garrison. How long ago had he seen him come out on the sidewalk? Three minutes? Four? No longer. Then Garrison was the killer. Either that or—

It was then that Casey heard the faint metallic sound. He looked at Austin, thinking he had made it, and saw Austin look at him with round, surprised eyes and knew he hadn't. He knew, too, that the sound had not come from this room, but from the one beyond.

He glanced at the connecting door and what he did then was the result of one of those spur-of-the-moment decisions that showed better than anything else could why Casey was rated the best camera in town. He didn't stop to worry about what might happen to him then; he wasn't even sure just what he was going to do; all he knew was that the noise he heard sounded peculiarly like a door closing. Someone had been in that other room. If that someone was the killer, if he was sneaking out—

Austin stood motionless, looking first at Casey and then at the door. Casey put his finger to his lips and stepped quickly past him. "Keep talking," he whispered, and with the tension winding up inside him, crossed swiftly to the door and palmed it.

"Maybe it's lucky for us we didn't come up here sooner," Austin said loudly.

He said other things but Casey didn't hear him as he twisted the knob silently and pushed on the door. Light followed him in, disclosing another room that seemed more sumptuous than the one he had just left. There were three doors here and Casey moved to the one giving on the hall, opening it as quietly as he could.

A growing stiffness slid along his joints as he peered out; then, still hearing vaguely Austin's continuing monologue, he stepped into the hall. The elevator stood as they had left it, flooding light into the corridor. At his elbow the rear stairs wound narrowly down into darkness. He tiptoed to the stairwell and listened.

He heard it then, the soft, hurried tapping. Below him. Growing rapidly less distinct, telling him he could not delay. He slipped off his oxfords, tucked them into his coat pockets, and started down, his stockinged feet making no sound as they sped over the stairs.

At the second-floor landing he paused to listen. There was no longer any tapping sound; for an instant there was no sound at all. Then a cold breeze spiraled up the stairs and slid along his ankles, and even as he felt it, he heard the solid click of a heavy door closing.

Casey ran the rest of the way. He groped in the darkness for the doorknob, found it, pushed against the steel door, and stepped outside. The door had a patent closing-device and he caught it just in time, a little angry that he should be so careless. He eased it shut and then, thinking of what might have happened, felt his first thrust of fear. Suddenly, with the blackness of the night all about him, he was cold and wondered about it until he realized he was sweating, that his nerves were tight and jumpy. It was so damned dark. He didn't know which way to turn and waited, breathless, half expecting a gun to start blazing at him.

When he heard no sound but the pounding of his heart, he stepped out, feeling the cobblestones under his feet, looking first one way and then the other until, presently, the street light at one end of the alley made an abrupt silhouette of some moving figure.

Instantly he felt all right again, and started along the alley, his confidence regained. The silhouette had become an overcoated figure now, a slightly bent and hurrying figure that moved out on the sidewalk and turned diagonally left. Not knowing yet whether it was a man or a woman, he loped after it.

He was still in the alley when he heard a car door slam. He was nearly to the sidewalk when he heard the motor start and he reached the street just as a small sedan angled swiftly from the curb diagonally across from him. After that he did not think but acted automatically, throwing his camera to his shoulder, seeing tile blue-white explosion of light as the flash bulb went off, catching a fleeting glimpse of the driver's face as he turned to look back; that was all, for the car, moving swiftly and with lights out, had disappeared around the corner.

Casey lowered the camera. He did not have much hope for that picture. It was too far away for one thing, and the face had been partly hidden by an upturned coat collar. If he couldn't identify that fragmentary glimpse, how could the camera capture it? He stood there disappointedly until he remembered his shoes; then he untied them and put them on.

Perry Austin was rocking gently in Endicott's high-back chair when Casey returned. He had a big cigar in his mouth and he removed it and flicked ashes on the rug before he spoke. "What happened?"

Casey told him.

Austin pursed his lips. "You crazy fool! That could have been the killer."

"Looks like it was." Casey reversed his film holder and got another flash bulb from his case.

"I've been looking around," Austin said. "This is quite a layout. The guy must have really been in the chips." He pushed a heavy humidor across the desk. "Have a cigar."

"Leave it alone," Casey growled. "You'll have your prints all over the joint."

Austin raised his brows. "That's right, I will." He looked down at the cigar, frowning. "How do you figure this, Flash?"

"I don't," Casey said. "That's for the cops. All I want is a couple of pictures."

"You going to call in?"

"Certainly." He gave Austin an irritated glance. Something about the man's attitude nettled him and he could not forget the fact that they had nearly trapped the killer. Looking back, he realized that he had taken a fool chance in trying to follow the man. If the fellow had known about it in time Casey might be stretched out in the alley as Endicott was on the floor. He went over to the dead man, walked around him until he got an angle he liked. He took a picture.

"Look." Austin had moved up to him. "This is your baby now. If I hang around I'll get tangled up with Homicide and maybe get stuck for a couple of hours here. If I'm going to get any shots at the Berkely I'd better shove off now."

"Okay," he said. "Stop at a drugstore and phone Lieutenant Logan; then I won't have to use this phone and maybe smudge up some prints for them. I'll tell him you were here with me, but Logan's all right, and he probably won't bother you until morning— And wait a minute," he said as Austin started for the door. "Take this with you." He handed over the exposed film holder. "You'll probably get back to the office before I do. But don't leave it around for somebody else to develop."

When the outer door closed and he heard the hum of the elevator he went to his plate case and got a fresh film holder and two more flash bulbs. He took two pictures of Endicott from different angles, put the film holder and burned-out bulbs in the case and got fresh ones. He looked about then, studying the furnishing of the room anew, and in, the end went back to the third room in the suite.

Here he turned on the light, noting that this room looked more like the library of some rich man's home than an office. There was a large fireplace, an oversized leather divan in front of it. Two of the walls were given over almost entirely to books. In addition to the hall door there were two others, one leading to a closet, the other to a private bath and dressing-room.

"Some layout," he said softly and then, with the words on his lips, he stiffened, holding his breath, listening. When the faintly humming sound which had attracted him continued, he stepped quickly to the hall door, opened it a crack, and listened. Sure, now, that the elevator was moving, he stayed there until he saw the light in the car flash past the crack under the door.

Now what? he thought, and closed the door. There was a chance that the passenger might be going to one of the offices across the hall. If not— He snapped off the room light as he heard the elevator door clang back. He went over to the door connecting with the center office, opened it a three-inch crack, and from the light that streaked in, looked again at the shutter and focus of the camera.

For the next second or two he could hear nothing at all. He waited. Presently a doorknob rattled. Then, too late, he realized that the crack he had opened would not permit him to view the opposite door, that he had better not risk further movement until he knew who was coming.

The quick, sharp gasp that followed was loud and startling. From where he stood he could see about one half of Endicott's body and for what seemed like minutes he saw nothing more. It was a temptation not to try and inch open the door a little farther, but he made himself wait, and presently a woman's white evening shoe came into view, and a long white dress—half of a dress, really— topped by a mink wrap.

He could not see her face, for when she moved again her back was toward him, and he realized suddenly that she had started away and was moving swiftly toward the door through which she had come. He stepped out just as that door opened, throwing up his, camera and calling, softly, "Hey."

The woman jerked to immobility, freezing with her hand on the knob. He could see her shoulders stiffen under the mink wrap and he waited, knowing that she would turn her head. She did, giving him a quick, over-the-shoulder glance. That's when Casey let off the flash gun, getting a fleeting glimpse of the blond hair, the startled, frightened eyes, and smooth, high-cheek-boned face. Even then the sight of her struck some responsive chord in his memory, but there was no time for anything more, because she had opened the door and was running through and slamming it behind her.

Casey started an instant later, crossing the room in long strides, hearing something scrape across the floor of the adjoining office. He grabbed for the knob, jerked at it, and went through the opening, seeing the fleeing silhouette framed in the door ahead. Then, as he leaped forward in the darkness, something caught his shin, dipping him, and he fell heavily, clumsily, as he tried to save the camera, knowing now what the scraping sound had been, that the woman had had the sense to spin a chair in his path as she fled.

He rolled to his knees, still protecting the camera, and stood up. Pain clamped round his shin and he hobbled over to the hall door, cursing bitterly. He went into the hall. The elevator was still there but he knew he'd never catch her now.

"Okay, sister," he said aloud. "But don't forget I got a picture, and this one's going to be good."

CHAPTER FOUR

CASEY GETS COOLED OFF

SERGEANT MANAHAN SAT on the edge of the desk smoking one of Stanford Endicott's cigars and, from the look on his broad ruddy face, enjoying it. The fingerprint man was assiduously dusting everything in sight that might conceivably hold a latent print, and the photographer, who had already taken pictures of the body and outlined it in chalk on the rug, was waiting for its removal, a tape measure in his hand. Lieutenant Logan stood by the examiner's physician while he completed his preliminary inspection.

"So here's once," the doctor said, "when I don't have to figure out the time of death for you."

Logan glanced at Casey, who had slumped down on the divan, and shook his head. "Just give me the slugs this time, doc."

The doctor stood up and packed his bag. "If they were all like this, life would be a lot simpler for me. I'll have him out of here in a few minutes."

Logan strolled over to Casey. "You and Perry Austin came up here, found the door to the outer office unlocked. You came in and here he was. That all?"

"No. There are a couple more things. I saw Nat Garrison."

Interest kindled in Logan's dark eyes. "Where?"

"Outside. Just coming out of the building."

"The hell you did! When?"

"Just as we drove up."

Logan put his hands on his hips and looked disgusted. "Well for— Why didn't you say so?"

"I just thought of it."

"Austin see him?"

Casey said he didn't know; he didn't think so. Logan stepped to the desk and scooped up the telephone. While he rumbled out the orders that would start the search for Nat Garrison, Casey studied him.

Tall, straight, and good-looking in a lean, dark way, Logan looked more like a successful young business man than a lieutenant of detectives, and only around the corners of his eyes and mouth was there any reflection of the ten years he had spent in the Department. He liked good clothes and kept them well, his linen always looked fresh, his shoes polished. He had the faculty of being as tough and hard as the occasion demanded, but this acquired hardness was not a quality that he flaunted indiscriminately, and he tried to keep in mind the fact that he was a public servant and not a dictator. Now, coming back to Casey again, his gaze was narrowed in thought.

"Garrison got out last week," he said. "He was one of the first guys Endicott defended after he left the D.A."

Casey tried to remember the details of that trial but they escaped him. He asked Logan about it.

"He shot up a guy," the lieutenant said. "He was collecting in the numbers racket and said the guy tried to hijack him. He had a previous conviction for assault, so the judge put him away. So he's our man, huh?"

"He's one of 'em."

Logan stopped rubbing his palms. "Who's the other?"

"I told you there were a couple things," Casey said. "Garrison was one, but there was another guy up here." He went on to tell what had happened, explaining how he had tried to follow the man, but not mentioning the photograph he had taken because he didn't know if it would be any good or not, and he wanted to be sure of what he had before getting Logan all steamed up.

"You think he was the killer?" Logan said as Casey finished. "You think you walked in on him?"

"He was hiding in that room."

"And you heard him go out and went out after him."

Sergeant Manahan had been listening from his perch on the desk. He came over, trailing cigar smoke. "You didn't recognize him, huh?"

Casey said he didn't, thinking again about the picture he had taken. He didn't like to hold out on Logan. He had known the lieutenant a long time, had worked with him often enough to know that in the long run he rated more favors and co-operation by playing ball than by trying to outsmart him. But this time he wasn't trying to outsmart anybody. He wanted to be sure what he had on the film. If it was a bust he'd forget it; if it turned out to be something, he could hand it over.

The door opened and two interns came into the room with a stretcher. Casey got a picture as they started out with their burden, and put the film holder in the plate case along with the two he had taken before Logan arrived. That's when he really began to think about the other film holder he had tucked in an inside pocket—the one of the woman in the mink coat.

Ever since that minute he had been trying to place her. He was positive he had seen her before and yet, somehow, he could not remember where. It was not a face he had seen somewhere casually either; she was someone of importance, someone he should know.

The more he thought about her the more annoyed he became. That fleeting glimpse of her when the flash bulb went off remained indelibly imprinted in his mind, but this time there was no load on his conscience insofar as Logan was concerned. To hand such a picture over now would be to put the woman under immediate suspicion and this was a responsibility Casey did not want to take. True, she had been at the scene of the murder and had not knocked when she entered, but it was unlikely that she would have come back if she had killed Endicott. No, he couldn't see her as the killer, and until he knew more about it he wasn't going to put her on a spot.

"Harry Nye's out here, Lieutenant."

"Nye?" Logan said.

"Yes, sir. He says Endicott asked him to stop by."

"He did, huh? Well, tell him to come in, Carney. We'll be glad to see him."

The officer opened the door and gave an order with a jerk of his head. A man loomed up behind him, hesitated, finally stepped past; then Casey put the name and face together and knew who the fellow was: Harry Nye, a private detective.

"I saw them carry that stretcher out," he said, "and asked who it was. I thought I'd better come up."

He had taken in the room with one swift glance as he spoke and now, as his gaze came to rest on Logan, Casey had a chance to size him up. He didn't know the man, although he'd heard of him, and what he'd heard had been neither good nor bad. Now he saw that he was a well-set-up fellow of 30 or so with close-cropped curly hair and a thin, pointed mustache. His face was big-boned, solid-looking, and his eyes seemed brown until, moving closer, Casey saw that they were like dark amber, flat, impersonal, revealing nothing.

"Any idea who did it?" Logan asked bluntly.

"Who did what?"

"Shot him. Twice. In the vest."

"So that was it. When?"

"About nine or a little after. Casey just missed it."

"Oh." Nye looked at Casey and back at Logan. "No, Lieutenant, I haven't any ideas at all."

"What did he want to see you about?"

"He didn't say."

"But you had an appointment."

"Not exactly. He called me up at dinner time and asked me to stop around ten if I wasn't busy."

Logan's manner became very patient. "Look, Nye. You worked for Endicott, didn't you?"

"On and off."

"Doing what?"

Nye shrugged and touched one side of his mustache with the knuckle of his index finger. "Lots of things. He needed an investigator and I guess he liked my work. When he told me to stop by, I thought maybe he had another job for me."

"Oh, sure," Logan said. "Sure. And when did you see him last?"

"About a week ago."

"That long?"

"He's been out of town," Nye said. "He didn't get back until late last night and then this morning they grabbed him on that bond rap."

"That must have been a big surprise to you."

"It was."

"How'd you know he was out of town?"

"I called the office here and they told me."

"He was in the middle on this bond business," Logan said, talking more to himself now than to Nye. "It probably wasn't the first time he peddled a haul to the insurance company, but it was the first time he got caught at it. He went to see the D.A. this afternoon after the hearing. Suppose he found out they had him cold and wanted to take a plea? If he sang a little it might be tough on the insurance company officials—one of them anyway—and it sure as hell would be tough on the mob that's been knocking off these banks. Once he really got talking, my guess is he could put plenty of guys away."

"And somebody figured that one out and stopped him," Nye said casually.

Logan bent an eye at him. "You can shove off for now," he said.

"Thanks." Nye buttoned his coat. "Sorry I can't help you any."

"I know you are," Logan said. "Sorry as hell."

Nye grinned at him, an unworried, imperturbable sort of grin. "You don't sound as if you'd got very far with this."

"We will, Harry," Logan said. "Just make sure you don't outsmart yourself."

He watched Nye go out, walked over to the windows, and stared into the night.

"One of these days we're going to nail that baby."

"For what?" Casey asked.

"I don't know. Maybe for this. Any private dick that lives as well as he does is out of bounds somewhere."

He went over to the desk, picked up his hat, then glanced at the photographer who was packing up his paraphernalia. He asked him if he had finished. The fellow said he had and Logan turned to the fingerprint man.

"What about you, Len? Get much?"

"I got millions of 'em," Len said. "The joint is plastered."

Logan said he'd see them in the morning and nodded to Manahan. "Let's go have a talk with Mrs. Endicott. Want to come, Flash?"

They rode over in the little police sedan, and when Manahan stopped in front of the apartment house on the Riverway, Casey started to haul out his plate case.

"Leave it," Logan said. "This will be tough enough without you popping a flash bulb in her face."

"I can take it with me, can't I?" Casey said.

"Leave it. What's the use of scaring her?"

Casey left the plate case as directed but he was still grumbling when he crossed the sidewalk to the Gothic entrance.

"She's not the scaring kind," he said. "I used to know her."

"Oh?"

"Sure. Before she married Endicott. She was a manikin."

"Good?" Manahan asked.

"Plenty," said Casey, "but expensive."

A marceled young man, who smelled of hair tonic, sat behind a quarter circle of desk in the lobby.

"Who shall I say is calling?" he demanded, when Logan asked the number of the Endicott apartment.

"You won't say anything, son," Logan said and flashed his shield. "Catch?"

"Yes, sir." The youth shrank one full size and called across the way to the Negro elevator boy. "Four-A, Sam."

Sam's eyes bugged at them and his collar rode up and down on his Adam's apple as he swallowed.

"Do you know if Mrs. Endicott's got company?" Logan asked.

"Seems like she has, sir. Yes, sir, I think she has— There you are, sir. Right over there."

He was pointing across the hall when the door swung back and as Casey stepped out he saw that there were but two apartments to the floor, a third door at the rear leading to the service doors and stairs.

Logan put his thumb on the mother-of-pearl button.

"You didn't send anyone over before?" Casey said. "You're going to give it to her cold?"

"It's the only decent way," Logan said.

The door opened up against a chain stop and Casey saw Louise Endicott's face in the opening. She saw him too, and slipped the chain and opened the door wider. Dance music from a radio or record player drifted from some room beyond and with it the sound of voices.

"Oh," she said, not sounding very cordial, though the recognition was there. "Hello, Jack."

"Hello, Louise."

She stood back from the door, watching Logan and Manahan uncertainly. She had a half-filled glass in her hand and wore a dress of sheer white jersey that contrasted sharply with her yellow-blond hair.

"Mrs. Endicott?" Logan said. "I'm Lieutenant Logan. Could we see you a minute?"

She blinked at that, but recovered quickly. "Why—I have some people here but—why, yes, Lieutenant. Come in, please."

She left them to move along the entrance foyer and closed the door, shutting off the music from the other room. She opened another door.

"We could go in here."

They followed her and Casey found himself in a small library. She shut the door and turned, and then Logan told her.

"I've some bad news. Your husband was killed a little while ago."

Like that he gave it to her, and Casey saw the facial muscles recoil, the sudden blanching of her skin so that the make-up stood out in crude patches. For just an instant she seemed to stagger; then she was fighting and her chin snapped up and her shoulders came back.

Casey pushed a chair toward her and she sat down. "Killed?" she said huskily.

"Murdered."

Her blue eyes were still wide, the mascaraed lashes pinned back. She caught her breath and said, "Oh," and pulled her gaze from Logan.

"Should I—do you want me to tell my friends to leave?"

"That won't be necessary," Logan said. "I just wanted to let you know and—well, ask a few questions if you feel up to it."

"All right." She leaned back in the chair and folded her hands in her lap, her face still pale but no longer chalky. "You'd better sit down, hadn't you?"

"Thanks."

He swiveled a straight-backed chair to face her. Casey went over and perched on the edge of a kneehole desk and Manahan leaned against the door.

"What time did he leave here?"

"About eight o'clock. But—please! Can't you tell me what happened?"

Logan said he could, and while he explained what he knew, Casey's mind folded back and he thought about the Louise Amory he had once known. He had taken her out just twice and that had been enough to tell him how things were. Even then Louise had known what she wanted, and she hadn't been a hypocrite either. Tall, deep-breasted, she had a showy type of beauty that hit you between the eyes until you realized it was pretty shallow and depended largely upon make-up. She wore good clothes and when you took her out it had to be to the best places and at a table where she could see and be seen. She was, quite frankly, out to better herself and whatever she did for you—if she was especially nice—was going to cost you something, one way or another. Well, she'd got what she wanted and now, at 28, she still had her figure and her blond beauty. Her mouth was a bit more selfish, a little more set at the corners, but you couldn't have everything.

"And you were here all evening?" Logan was saying. "What about servants?"

"There's only a cook and a houseboy now. She sleeps home and I—I let the boy go at eight tonight."

"When did these—friends drop in?"

"Just a little while ago." She glanced at her wrist watch. "About ten."

Logan asked if he could have their names, and took them down in a little book. There were only four of them, two men and two women, none of whom was familiar to Casey. Logan stood up. He asked her if she knew anyone who might have wanted to kill her husband, and she said no, that's what made it so awful. Logan said he was sorry, and thanked her for her help. He said nothing more until they were down on the sidewalk.

"I've heard that Bernie Dixon's been giving her a play lately. I wonder how she was taking this rap against her husband."

Casey thought about Dixon as he crossed the sidewalk, remembering now that he had heard the same thing. Bernie Dixon ran the Club Berkely, and those columnists who had the run of the club referred to him in print as a restaurateur and night-club impresario. Ten years ago he'd been a New York gangster and although all that had been forgotten by the best people who now flocked to his Club and fought for ringside tables, for Casey's dough he was still a gangster.

He got in the back seat of the sedan, reaching for his plate case as Manahan pressed the starter. The case wasn't on the seat nor on the floor and he tapped Logan's shoulder.

"Hand me the plate case."

"It's in the back."

Casey searched the floor. "It ain't here. It must be up front."

"You had it," Logan said. "You started to get out with it and I told you to leave it."

Manahan let out the clutch and Casey yelled at him. "Wait, damn it!"

Manahan stopped the car with a jerk. He looked at Casey; so did Logan. Casey said, very quietly now, "Is it up there?"

"No. I told you—" That's as far as Logan got. He saw the grim twist of the big photographer's mouth, the ridged line of his jaw. "Gone?" he said in slow bewilderment.

Casey just looked at him, trying to put down the unreasoning anger that churned inside him. Now that he knew it was gone, now that the shock was over, the bitterness was on him hot and implacable.

"Just leave it here," he mocked stiffly. "It'll be all right. Oh, yes. Hell, yes. This is a police car, boys. Can't you see the shield on the door?—Those shots I took of Endicott were in that case. So was my camera." He gave Manahan's arm a jab. "Well, go on. I want to report this. Let's go find a cop."

Logan made no reply to these sarcasms and Casey didn't subside much as the car started off. "Boy, if this isn't something," he said. "We'll put it in a box on page three. You can cut it out and hang it on your wall, Logan."

He said other things too, pointless things, because he was sore. And all through it Logan didn't say a word. He waited until Casey ran out of breath before he looked back and said, "What did you have in that case besides those plates and that camera?"

That cooled Casey off; it cooled him off plenty. Not until then did he think of the two pictures that were *not* in the case: the one of the woman, the one of the man in the sedan. One of these he had tucked away in his pocket; the other Perry Austin had.

"Nothing," he said shortly, and kept right on thinking. Suppose Logan was right? Ordinarily his exposed film holders would be in that plate case. If someone wanted them bad enough he might hang around outside Endicott's offices—or have someone do it for him— and wait for Casey to come out. But Casey had come out with two cops, had driven away and left that plate case in the car— He leaned back in the corner, no longer angry, but troubled, brooding, the conviction growing that Logan *was* right.

CHAPTER FIVE

PURE DYNAMITE!

THERE WAS NO ONE ELSE in the studio when Casey got back to the *Express* building. It was not quite eleven o'clock and he looked first on his desk to see if Austin had left the other film holder for him. When he could not find it, he took the holder with the picture of the woman in it and went into one of the darkroom cubicles.

He knew he had a good negative when he took it from the hypo but he still did not know who his subject was and he stood impatiently before the warm-air fan as he waited for the film to dry. He was still there when he heard someone in the anteroom. He left the clips on the film and went out to take a look.

The man who stood there carried about 260 or 270 pounds on a five-foot-ten frame. His hair was thick and gray under his pushed-back felt, his face was heavy and pasty-colored and he did not look very well in spite of his size. He was past 60 and until three years ago when he had been sent to prison for manslaughter, he had worked for the *Express*. His name was Jim Bishop.

"Hello, Flash." He was puffing noisily, as though he had been hurrying. "Hoped I'd find you."

"Hello, Jim. You're out late, aren't you?"

"Sort of." Jim Bishop took off his hat and ran his hand around the sweatband. He got out a handkerchief and mopped his face, though the room was not warm.

"What's on your mind?" Casey asked, aware of the other's nervousness now and wondering about it.

"A picture."

Casey let his brows come up but said nothing.

"A picture you took tonight. I think it was you, anyway. You were in Endicott's office, weren't you?"

Casey leaned against the desk, eyes narrowing. "How'd you know?"

Bishop sighed. He swallowed, and a look of relief struck his puffy face. "I thought it was you from the way she described you."

"Oh." Casey went around the desk and sat down, thinking fast and getting nowhere. "I don't get it, Jim," he said. "Where do you come in? Who was she?"

"You don't know?"

Casey shook his head. "But there are a lot of things I don't know. Come on." He got up suddenly and led the way into the semi-darkness of the printing-room.

He could hear Bishop waddling behind him, but he did not look at him then; instead he took the clips off the film, went over to the enlarger, slid a piece of paper in the easel. He put the film in the machine and snapped on the light, knowing from long experience just about how much exposure that particular print would need. He snapped off the light, slipped out the paper, and slid it into the developing-tray. Behind him he heard Bishop say, "Is that it?"

Casey did not answer. He took another piece of paper and repeated the performance, giving this one another second or two of exposure and taking the first from the developer and putting it in water. Presently, when he had both prints in the fixing bath, he pulled out one and held it under the safe-light. One look was all he needed. He put the print back in the hypo and turned, folding his arms.

"Lyda Hoyt," he said softly.

"Yes," Bishop said. "I thought you knew. I thought—" He did not finish the sentence, or if he did Casey did not hear him. There was a curious tingling along his nerve ends now, and over and over his brain was saying, *Lyda Hoyt, Lyda Hoyt.* No wonder she'd looked familiar, since she was the best-known musical-comedy star of the day. He'd seen her on the stage a half-dozen times in the past five years, had taken her picture once or twice at press interviews. Her current show—she'd had it on the road for many months and was winding up at the Shubert this week—was last season's hit, *Crimson Blossoms.*

Casey thought of this and other things, remembering something else no less important. Lyda Hoyt had announced her engagement only a week ago to Grant Forrester, and the Forresters, some wag had once said, spoke only to the Cabots and the Lowells— Casey glanced down at the two prints in the fixing bath. They were face up, the image of the woman sharp and clear and, in the foreground, the head and shoulders of the murdered Stanford Endicott.

Pure dynamite, he thought. What he said was, "Tell me about it, Jim." He pulled a stool in front of Bishop. "Maybe we'd better talk in here, in case somebody walks in while these prints are washing."

Bishop ignored the stool. He moved to the doorway and glanced toward the anteroom. He came back and spoke in measured tones. "I have to have them, Flash."

"Why?"

"Why?" Bishop's mouth dropped, making four chins instead of three. "But, good God, man! Suppose someone got ahold of a print. Think what—"

"That's not what I meant," Casey said. "How do you fit? Why should Lyda Hoyt call you?"

"I'm her uncle."

"What?" Casey peered at him. "You're what?"

"That's right. She phoned me right after the curtain came down. You can imagine how she feels. She was frantic. She didn't know what to do and luckily I thought to ask her what the fellow looked like that took the picture. Then I knew it had to be you. I thought if I told you how things were—"

He broke off again and tried to read the answer in the big photographer's face, but Casey was still sorting out tangled fibers of his thoughts. It would be a simple matter to tell Bishop that he could have the negative and prints. In the end Casey knew he would probably hand them over because he did not think Lyda Hoyt had killed Stanford Endicott, and he knew what the consequences would be if one of those prints found its way into the wrong hands.

Yet, over a period of years, there had developed in Casey a curious complex about the pictures he took. Many a time he had found himself with some shot that might have caused trouble for an innocent person; more often he had pictures of men and women not so innocent. Very often they were well-known people—women caught in gambling raids, men in night clubs with women not their wives. Those people came to him and begged for those pictures and almost always he handed them over, since they did not constitute news and could do no one but a scandal sheet any good.

But always before he gave up the picture he had to be sure. He had to know the circumstances because there were many who objected to having their picture taken on purely personal grounds. If he gave back the picture of everyone who protested he would have been fired long ago. No. The problem was one of selection and he was careful because once a negative had been destroyed there was no replacing it. In one or two instances he had been tricked, had been sold on a phony story and, not knowing the facts, had passed up a sensational and newsworthy picture. It was this same suspicion that made him question Jim Bishop now. There had been a murder tonight and Casey wanted all the answers he could get.

"What's the rest of it, Jim?" he said finally. "I guess you can have them, but I'd like to know what the score is. This uncle business—that's kind of hard to take."

"Sure." Bishop mopped his face again. "Sure it is, Flash. She's my dead sister's kid. It goes back about twelve years. Up till then I'd see her once in a while when her mother brought her to New York—I was on the *Standard* there for years, you know—and then her mother died and she went someplace with her father; someplace out on the coast. I lost track of them. I had some tough luck of my own and got to boozing and got fired and came up here and got on at the *Express*. Five years ago she called me up. I fell over. She was Lyda Hoyt, the actress, the new sensation direct from London."

He paused for breath and went on. "She'd had me traced. She's the one that looked me up, not the other way around. I'd seen her picture in the papers and magazines and didn't even know it was her. There's a lot of difference in a woman's looks between 18 and 25 —she's 30 now—and as a kid she was fat and pudgy and no style and now she's—well, you know. I never told anyone. You know how it is. The gag was that she was English and an orphan—which she was—and that was good publicity. She got around in society here and there and they had her engaged to Lord this and Count that, and that was good for her shows.

"It would've been swell, huh, for the papers to find out she wasn't English at all, and that she had a fat slob like me for an uncle. She used to sneak out to see me when she was in town, and she'd write and send me things, but nobody knew, and that was the way it should be. Now—well, you know. She's going to marry Grant Forrester. Suppose anyone found out her uncle had killed a man in a drunken brawl and done two years for manslaughter?"

Casey thought of a lot of things then. He'd been filling in gaps as Bishop unfolded the story and now those things fitted together in his mind. Bishop had come up from New York ten years previous to take a job on the *Express* at probably about one-third of his former salary. He'd been over 50 then, and they knew he'd been fired and put him on the police assignment, warning him to cut down on the booze. He straightened out then, and went along in fine shape until one day he'd dived in the river to pull out a kid who'd overturned a skiff. The river police had fished Bishop out more dead than alive and for a month it was doubtful whether he would pull through. At his age the strain had been too much for his heart and from then on he had to watch himself and take things easy.

Right away he began to put on weight. They gave him a job on the copy desk and everything was all right until that night about three years ago when he'd got in an argument with some fellow in the back room of a Washington Street bar. They hadn't even known each other, these two, but they were both liquored up and the fellow swung at Bishop and Bishop had slugged him with a bottle and killed him, hit him three or four times before they stopped him. Sanford or Sanburn, the man's name was. Something like that. And when the police looked him up they found he had a record and two convictions for armed robbery. That and the fact that witnesses testified the fellow was a complete stranger, got Bishop off with a light sentence.

He'd been out a year now, living on a small income, playing chess when he could find an opponent, drinking a little beer on occasion but keeping quiet. There had been one more heart attack that nearly finished him but he was always cheerful.

"Yeah," Casey said thoughtfully. "I guess it wouldn't be so good for her, Jim. Well—" He took the prints from the washer and rolled them and put them on the dryer. He slipped the negative from the enlarger. "Let's go in the other room."

He sat down at his desk and Bishop lowered himself into a chair with a series of wheezes. Casey tossed the negative in front of him. "What about tonight? Did you know she was going to see Endicott?"

"No."

"You don't know what she wanted?"

Bishop shook his head. "She went and you caught her, that's all I know. I was home playing chess with Emerson. You know we generally get together once a week." Casey nodded. Emerson was the librarian, in charge of the morgue, a pensioner of the *Express*. "And I got her call about eleven. I came right over."

Casey got up and went in for the two prints. When he came back he gave one to Bishop and studied the other, seeing something now that he had not noticed before. Lyda Hoyt was in perfect focus, her eyes wide and startled, her hand on the door. In front of her, a little fuzzy but still identifiable, was part of Endicott's body. Off to one side, atop a low bookcase that stood adjacent to the door, was an electric clock. The hands pointed to 9:35.

"What're you going to do with them, Jim?" Casey indicated the negative and print Bishop held.

"Why—destroy them. Good God! You don't think I'd leave them around, do you?"

"Then I'll keep this one."

Bishop looked up quickly, his glance puzzled. Casey put the extra print in his desk drawer and locked it.

"Have you seen her show?"

Bishop shook his head, still puzzled.

"Neither have I," Casey said. "It looks like she came over to Endicott's during intermission—it's only about five minutes away and she must have figured there was time enough."

"I still don't get you," Bishop said.

"Without that picture she might not have an alibi, Jim. It's a long shot, but it could happen. Suppose the police *did* find out? It might be sort of handy to be able to prove just when she was there. This shot with that clock in it will do it."

"But you know when she was there."

"Sure. And probably I'll still be alive tomorrow and the next day and next year. But why take the chance I won't be?" He shook his head and grinned. "Don't worry about it, but I'm funny that way. Once you destroy a negative and its prints you're out of luck. I'm keeping this one until I'm sure."

Bishop pulled himself to his feet with an effort. He looked at the negative and print in his hand. He reached for an ash tray, found a match, touched the flame to the corner of the negative and the print.

"Thanks, Flash." He offered his hand. "I'll tell her. All I can say is thanks, but we won't forget it, ever."

He turned and waddled out and Casey watched him go, wondering why he had to be so damn cautious about turning over that extra print. Nothing was going to happen to him, and there wasn't a chance that anyone would find out Lyda Hoyt had been in Endicott's office. Still—stranger things than that had happened. Who would have thought someone would have lifted his plate case right out of a police car—?

The instant the thought came to him his eyes clouded. He felt for a cigarette, lit it, walked over to the windows. For a minute or two he stood there, staring sightlessly out across the roof tops, his broad face grave and resentment undermining his thoughts.

Suppose Lyda Hoyt had telephoned Bishop earlier? Suppose he had hurried to the building housing Endicott's offices? There'd be police cars out front then and he would have to wait. Suppose he had waited—for Casey. He could have tailed the police sedan, could have easily lifted the plate case while Casey was up with Logan and Manahan and Mrs. Endicott. It would be even easier that way than coming and asking for it. Only when the plate case was inspected the right picture was missing— A thing like that would force Bishop to come here.

He sat down at his desk and picked up the telephone. Half-ashamed, yet driven by some inner stubbornness that would not rest until he knew the truth, he asked the night operator to try Mr. Emerson's residence.

"John," he said presently. "This is Casey. I'm trying to locate Jim Bishop. Isn't this your night for chess?"

"Oh, hello," Emerson said. "Yes, Flash. Yes, we played chess tonight."

"When?"

"Well—I guess I got there at eight-thirty."

"Play long?"

"Till pretty near eleven. We were on our second game. I'd've had him checkmated in three more moves, only the phone rang. He said he had to go out."

"Oh," Casey said, still fishing. "You went out with him, huh? He didn't say where he was going?"

"No. He dropped me here at my place. It was just about eleven then. Said he had to see a fellow."

Casey thanked the man and hung up, feeling a little sheepish about the whole thing. Well, that was that. If Bishop was out of circulation from 8:30 until nearly 11:00 he hadn't stolen any plate case between a quarter and half past ten.

"Then who the hell did?" he said finally.

CHAPTER SIX
TIED UP WITH MURDER

CASEY SAT THERE AT HIS DESK for quite a while before he got the matter of the missing plate case out of his mind, and after that he began to think about Perry Austin and the other film holder he was supposed to deliver.

"Probably still clowning around down at the Berkely," he said under his breath, and before he could continue with the subject the telephone rang.

It was Blaine. He said, "I want to see you," and hung up.

Casey went upstairs and crossed to the city desk. Blaine gave him a quick gray stare and went back to editing a piece of copy. "Where've you been?"

"Down to Endicott's."

"What about pictures?"

"I got one of him—dead."

Blaine looked up, interested now but nothing showing in his voice. "Just one?"

Casey thought about the plate case. To hell with it. Alibis were no good. *How* he got pictures was Casey's affair and if he ran into grief that was his tough luck.

"Yeah," he said. "Just one."

"Where is it?"

"Austin's got it."

"Why?"

Casey told him, deliberately, flatly.

"You walked in right after he'd been shot?" Blaine said. "You and Austin. Why didn't you call in?"

"The place was crawling with reporters by the time Logan got there," Casey said. "What're you crabbing about? All I'm supposed to do is take pictures." He turned away, stopped. "Austin's your boy, isn't he? Well, when he gets back you'll get your picture."

He kept on going this time, detouring past the studio to get his hat and coat and then tramping down the street two blocks to a bar that charged ten cents more a drink and gave you atmosphere for it. Andre's, it was called. There were lots of carpet and chromium and red-leather stools and black-topped tables. There were not more than a half-dozen customers about and Casey took a stool at the bar, ordering rye and soda.

When the drink came he poured the rye, tasted the mixture. He lit a cigarette and emptied his glass. He was just about to order a refill when there was a flurry of movement around the entrance and three men came in. Casey saw that much, but there was no recognition in his glance until he heard the major domo greet them.

"Good evening, Mr. Forrester, good evening."

Casey's head came round. They were marching toward him now, three stalwart-looking fellows in top hats and tails, looking neither right nor left but at him.

The two bartenders took up the chant. "Good evening, Mr. Forrester. Good evening, Mr. Forrester. Good evening, Mr. Van Doren."

Casey pegged the three of them then. The big fellow in the center he recognized as Grant Forrester, the fiancé of Lyda Hoyt. The blond on his right was his younger brother, Russ, and the third man was a cousin, Bill Van Doren. The way they carried themselves, the way they wore those rich man's clothes told you they'd been doing it a long time.

Opposite him they broke ranks, Van Doren going to the stool beyond and the two Forresters flanking Casey on the other side. The bartender flipped paper serviettes down in front of them and said, "Yes, sir. What will it be, gentlemen?"

"Black Label," Van Doren said, "and Perrier."

"Three," Grant Forrester said. He looked at Casey. "You're Casey, aren't you? Yes. And give Mr. Casey another—whatever it is he's having."

Casey looked one way and then the other, adding things up fast and getting only one answer: Lyda Hoyt had not only telephoned her uncle, but she had tipped off Grant Forrester as well.

"We'd like to see you," Grant Forrester said.

"Swell," said Casey. He looked the other in the eye. "And now what?"

"Oh, I mean outside. After you've finished your drink."

"Drinks. I may be here quite a while."

"You can come back—I think."

"I like it here," Casey said.

Forrester shrugged and nodded to Van Doren. "All right. If that's the way you want it."

"You're going to drag me out, huh?"

"Don't you think we can?"

"Yeah," Casey said, "I think you can. Starting even, I might give you an argument, but we're not starting even. If you start something everybody in the place will swear I slugged you first. You're Mr. Forrester. You carry weight. People believe you and even if they don't they'll say they do."

"That's one way of looking at it," Forrester said.

"It's the only sensible way of adding it up and you know it. Because after the brawl I wind up in the can with a few lumps and all you'll get is the lumps. Still,"—he watched the bartender put down his drink and drank some of it—"I might take you on just for the hell of it. What do you want?"

"The picture you took of Miss Hoyt," Forrester said.

Casey looked at the bartenders. They were giving him the worried eye and he knew they could hear what was being said. Well, that's what happened when you gave pictures away. He couldn't tell Forrester the truth now. He couldn't tell him about Bishop because he didn't dare betray the secret that Lyda Hoyt and her uncle had kept. And if he couldn't tell about Bishop he couldn't tell Forrester what he'd done with the print and negative. He glanced at the bartenders again; they still looked worried in an expectant sort of way.

"All right," Casey said, "I'll go out with you."

"Splendid. Shall we drink up?"

"By all means. Then we can have another."

"But—"

Casey turned on the innocent eye, the candid manner. "You bought. Shouldn't I have the privilege of returning the compliment?"

"Well—" Forrester cocked an eye at his brother, looked back at Casey, and a gleam of humor fought its way through the disturbed darkness of his eyes. "You win," he said and ordered again.

From then on Casey liked him, and, studying him covertly, he quickly decided that Forrester would be no bargain even without the support of his brother and cousin. About 35, Casey thought; as tall as he was and weighing about 190. His hair was a medium brown, his eyes gray-blue and clear and direct. He played six-goal polo, had boxed in college, and once went three rounds in a charity exhibition with Braddock. It wasn't just his rich man's clothes and manners, either, that impressed; it was something in his eye, something about the cut of his jaw that told you that although he was accustomed to the best he could battle the worst down to the finish without saying uncle.

He shifted his gaze to Van Doren. Solid, dark, not so tall. And the brother, Russ—he was not more than 26 or 27, blonder, engaged to Senator Waverly's daughter. Casey shook his head absently. What a spot Lyda Hoyt had picked to have her picture taken—

The sedan at the curb, its bumper practically touching a fire plug, looked 25 feet long. Van Doren got in behind the wheel and Casey climbed in between the two brothers, wondering what he was going to say.

He couldn't say a word about Bishop. He had no intention of telling about the one print in his desk; to do so would only make Forrester demand the negative. There wasn't much use in stalling or saying that the film didn't come out.

"Where is it?" Forrester asked as the car got under way.

"I haven't got it."

"Oh?" Forrester's voice got polite but thin. "What happened to it?"

"Nothing."

"I thought you were going to be reasonable," Forrester said. "What is it you want, money?"

Casey felt the surge of hot anger in his neck. He sat up. Then he got an idea and cooled off again.

"Look," he said. "I saw Lyda Hoyt tonight. All I had to do was tell the police—and Lieutenant Logan who was detailed to the case is a friend of mine. Did I tell him?"

"Why—I don't know."

"The hell you don't. If I had you'd have heard about it hours ago. Logan would have been waiting for her when she walked off the stage."

"Yes. I suppose that's true." Forrester flexed his lips. "But just the same. That photograph—"

"It's like this," Casey said, liking his idea better all the time. "I haven't got it. It hasn't been developed. I gave it to a fellow named Perry Austin. Because I knew I'd be tied up with the police. He didn't know what was in the film holder but I told him to hang on to it and not develop it or hand it over to anyone but me. I haven't seen him since. For all I know he's out on some assignment."

"You say he works with you?"

"Sure. And I'm sort of the boss in the studio. He'll do what I tell him. So why don't you forget it? Nobody's going to get that picture but me and if I wanted to throw any curves I'd have done it before now. Forget it. Don't worry about it."

When Casey talked like that, you believed him and Forrester said so. "I believe you," he said. "After all you *could* have told the police, as you say. I'm very grateful that you didn't and I— well, I apologize for dragging you around this way. It was a crazy idea but I didn't know what else to do— Well, thanks a lot, old man. I shan't forget it. Is there any place you'd like to go? Back to Andre's?"

Casey glanced out the window as the car sped along, saw that they were within a block of Austin's apartment, and decided to stop and see if he was home. "This'll do," he said. "Right here on the corner. I want to see a fellow."

Van Doren pulled up at the curb and Casey got out. Grant Forrester leaned forward, offering his hand. "Thanks again—and when can you give me the picture?"

"By tomorrow afternoon," Casey said. "Call me some time after noon."

He watched the sedan roll away and started down the street, well pleased with his subterfuge. Some time during the morning he'd make a copy of that picture he had in his desk. When he developed the negative of that copy, Forrester probably wouldn't be able to tell it from the original.

Casey played with these thoughts as he glanced at the row of brownstone fronts that marched along with him in the darkness. He had never been in Austin's apartment, but he had dropped him off here several times and when he entered the building he found the entryway lighted and got the apartment number from name cards along the wall.

Beyond the inner door, the interior had been modernized, but long old-fashioned stairs hugged one wall, and he went up whistling softly, his hand trailing on the polished bannister. Then, just as he turned the corner at the second floor, he saw the girl.

She was coming toward him from an angle, as if she had just stepped from one of the apartments ahead. He had only a fleeting glimpse of her face before she started to pass him, and although the light was bad, there was something familiar about the tweed suit and the angle of the tapered face that made him move in front of her so that she had to stop or bump into him.

"Hello," he said, and then she looked up and he knew he had been right, that this was the girl who had come to the studio asking for Austin. "Isn't he in?"

For one brief instant her face seemed white and startled, but she composed it quickly and said, "Oh, I didn't recognize you— No, he didn't answer," she said, and stepped past. Then she was going down the stairs and he stood there, grunting softly, wondering who she was and why she was so interested in Austin.

The apartment he sought was one of the two at the front and he knocked at the door, waited, knocked again. The lock, he saw, was of the old-fashioned type and he stooped and put his eye to the key-hole. When he found nothing but blackness beyond he sighed and went back downstairs, a little annoyed with himself for not taking the girl's word. In the foyer he glanced at his wrist watch. It was just 12:20. He went out on the sidewalk, glancing up at the apartment again as he tramped off down the street.

It was a seven- or eight-minute walk to the *Express* and Casey went directly to the studio. The anteroom was empty and he slid out of his coat and tossed it on the desk; then, as he pulled out his chair to sit down, he saw the plate case.

At first he didn't believe it and stood staring, a frown biting into his brow and his eyes puzzled. Finally he realized he was staring and, with mounting incredulity, lifted it to the desk, fumbled with the straps, opened it. Then he was sure it was his and quickly yanked out the camera, inspecting it to be sure it was all right. It was. But there was no film holder in it; no exposed film holders in the case itself. "What the hell!" he said.

He looked across the room, brows still warped but seeing nothing. Presently his gaze came back to the camera and case. He kicked the chair out a little farther and sat down. That's when he noticed the center drawer of his desk. It was open about an inch. The wood around the lock was chewed and the lock itself was bent.

The impact of this discovery was like a physical jolt and he grabbed for the drawer and pulled it open. He pawed through it again and again with sweaty hands.

He searched the other drawers but even as he did so he knew it was no use. He had put that picture of Lyda Hoyt in the center drawer. It was gone. Whoever had stolen his plate case had found out the picture was not in that case and had come back with it to resume the search.

Casey sat back and the stiffness went out of him. His face was dark and brooding under its film of moisture. He thought of Jim Bishop and the things he had told Grant Forrester, and a bitterness was in his mouth and throat as he tried to think and then tried not to, when he found the result so discouraging.

He was still sitting there, a burly grim-faced man, when the sound of whistling came along the hall and Tom Wade swung into the room. "Hi, big shoot," he said airily. He slid his plate case along the floor. "Boy, did I have an assignment tonight. The West Roxbury Players—and not bad either. There was a dame there—" He broke off and walked round to look at Casey. "What's *your* trouble?"

"Go 'way," said Casey, not looking up.

Wade shrugged and began whistling again. He opened his plate case, took out a couple of film holders and started toward the dark-room corridor, his heels rapping on the composition floor. He went through the doorway. Suddenly the rap of his heels stopped and Casey heard what sounded like a gasp. Then Wade yelled. "Flash!"

An icicle ripped along Casey's spine and he jumped up, knocking over the chair. There was something in that yell he had never heard before and he leaped for the doorway, his throat dry and heart pounding.

Wade stood stock-still on the threshold of the printing-room and Casey couldn't stop in time and slammed into him, knocking him aside. Wade never said a word; he just stood there looking ahead of him at the floor. Then Casey saw why. Crumpled there in the semi-darkness of the room lay a man, his topcoat bunched about his waist, his hat half on and half off his head.

Casey sucked in his breath and stepped forward, going to one knee. The man was on his side, his head on one outstretched arm. "Finell!" he breathed.

"Good God!" Wade said. "What—is he—"

He didn't finish the question but Casey knew what he meant and got the hat off and felt a wrist and said, "No. He's alive."

"What's the matter with him?"

Worry and anxiety made Casey's voice ragged and stiff. "How the hell do I know?" He got his arms under Finell's knees and shoulder, lifted him easily. "Get his coat off."

The man's arms hung limp and it was a simple matter for Wade to slip off the topcoat; then Casey carried Finell into the lighted anteroom, ordered Wade to make a bundle of the coat, and stretched out the inert form on the floor, the coat under his head. That was when he saw the ugly bruise near the top of the skull and knew that Finell, the redheaded photographer that everybody liked, had been slugged.

"Get on the phone," he said. "Get a doctor up here."

And even as he spoke he knew that this thing that had happened to Finell was tied up with him—with his stolen plate case, and jimmied desk, and the picture he had kept because he thought he was being so smart.

CHAPTER SEVEN
A COUPLE OF HOODS

THEY WATCHED THE DOCTOR examine Finell—Casey and Wade and Blaine and the two ambulance men who stood in the doorway. Wade was hunched over in a chair, his elbows on his knees, his round face still pale and miserable. Blaine paced the floor in tight little circles, his hands behind his back and his thin, angular features tight and hard. Casey stood over the doctor, legs spread, fists thrust deep in his coat pocket. No one said anything; no one had said anything in the past three or four minutes.

"I think he'll be all right, but we never know about head injuries until we get some X-rays. Probably only a concussion—you say he had his hat on and that may have saved him from a fracture—but I can't be sure."

"How long will he be our?" Casey said.

"I can't tell that either. Five minutes, five hours, a day." He shrugged and put on his coat, nodding to the ambulance men who came forward and lifted Finell gently to the stretcher.

"We'll go with him," Casey said. He looked at Wade. "You take my car and I'll go along in the ambulance."

He started for his coat and Blaine took his arm. "Why would anyone slug him?"

Casey looked down into the narrowed gray eyes. "He must have walked in on somebody who didn't belong here."

Blaine watched the stretcher being carried out. He told the doctor to see that Finell had the best of everything, but he still held to Casey's arm. "Let Wade ride the ambulance," he said. "You can go along in a few minutes."

Casey thought it over and nodded to Wade. "Okay. Take his coat with you. I'll be out."

Blaine waited until they were alone. "What would anybody want to slug him for?" he asked again.

Casey thought he knew but he couldn't tell Blaine the whole story and there was another possibility. He asked about it. "What was his assignment? When did he leave here?"

"I called him about ten-forty. A fire in the South End."

Casey went to Finell's plate case—they had found it in the printing-room—and opened it. There were two film holders exposed, indicating Finell had taken four pictures. That they were here proved that Casey's alter native was wrong; Finell had not been slugged because of them.

"Somebody broke into my desk tonight," he said, and showed Blaine the damaged lock. "I think Finell walked in on the guy—or guys—that did it. Somebody put the slug on him and dragged him into the other room."

"What was in your desk?"

"Lots of things."

"You know what I mean."

Casey was in no mood to argue, nor did he feel he could tell the truth about the picture of Lyda Hoyt, even to Blaine. He could not help feeling that he was indirectly responsible for what happened to Finell, and this thought served only to heighten his resentment.

"Somebody swiped my plate case tonight," he said and went on to explain what had happened, how he had found the case here when he came back for the second time.

"What pictures were in the case?" Blaine asked.

"The ones I took at Endicott's."

"And what else?"

Casey stifled an angry outburst and deliberately waited until he could speak reasonably. "If I knew all the answers I wouldn't be horsing around here arguing with you," he said finally.

"You didn't tell me about the plate case before."

"Because you're the guy who hates alibis. You want pictures from me."

"And so far I haven't got any."

"You will," Casey said. "When Austin shows up."

Blaine stepped back. He wasn't satisfied, not by a long way was he satisfied. His mouth was thin and sardonic and his gray eyes were speculative and intent.

"All right," he said, and picked up Finell's film holder. "Develop those for me before you go, will you?"

When Casey had sent Finell's prints up to Blaine he came back to the studio and for the first time in an hour or more began to think about Perry Austin and that film holder he was apparently carrying around with him. Where the hell was he? And why hadn't he left the film holder here as he was told?

There was no answer to these questions, but thinking of them raised another. Could there be any connection between the theft of the plate case and that picture he had taken of the man he had followed from Endicott's apartment? In any case the thing to do was find Austin and see what was on the film.

He looked at his watch. It was too late to go down to the Club Berkely; the place would be closed. Nevertheless he picked up the telephone and asked the operator to get the number. Someone might be there. Someone was.

"Yes?" An accented voice came to him. "Dominic speaking."

Casey identified himself. "Is Bernie Dixon there?" No, Bernie Dixon had just left. "Well, look. You know Perry Austin, don't you?"

"Oh, yes."

"What time did he leave?"

Dominic didn't know. Yes, he remembered seeing Mr. Austin earlier in the evening but there had been a big crowd and he had been very busy and—

"Yes, sure," Casey said. "Okay, Dominic." He hung up, scowled at the instrument, glanced at his wrist watch again. That was the hell of this town. The bars closed down too early and you never knew where to look for anyone at this hour except home. Still, there was one place that might be open at this hour—and it was the kind of place that Dixon patronized.

He picked up the telephone again and called Dixon's apartment. When the houseboy finally answered and said Dixon had not returned, Casey called the hospital. After some delay he got Wade.

"How is he?"

"Pretty good, so they tell me."

"Conscious?"

"No. But no fracture. His condition's good and they say he's going to be okay."

"Swell," Casey said. "When he comes around maybe he can tell us who slugged him. Stick around awhile, will you?"

"But I thought you—"

"I was, but I can't," Casey said. "I got to look for Perry Austin. I'll call you back."

The Avenue was deserted now and the traffic lights along its tree-lined length had been turned off. There was a block or so of sedate and modern apartments, an occasional one thereafter, but for the most part there were only ancient houses of brick and stone that looked stiff and unpromising in the shadows. Some were empty, some had the windows boarded up or shuttered, almost all were dark.

The house Casey sought was in the middle of the block but the management preferred to have its patrons leave their cars distributed over a wide area rather than have them bunched near the entrance, so Casey pulled the convertible to a stop, just beyond the intersection and walked the rest of the way.

He stepped into a small entryway and at the same time the door at the opposite end opened and shut and a trim, smooth-faced youth was there to meet him.

"Your card, please?"

"I lost it," Casey said, unbuttoning his coat.

The youth's eyes flickered and the lids came down. He had an olive skin and patent-leather hair and a bulge under the left arm of his dinner jacket.

"Sorry." He leaned back against the door. "You have to have a card, mister."

"Ring Nick."

The fellow shook his head and his lips moved in what might have been a smile. Casey moved up a step and grinned and reached for the push button in the wall. The fellow made a grab for his arm and Casey swiveled and pinned him against the door and pressed the button.

He stepped back, still grinning. The youth had his hand behind him now and his hair was mussed. His eyes had sparks in them.

"If you got a sap in that pocket you'd better leave it there," Casey said, and then a square metal peephole slid back and a hooked nose and close-set eyes looked out.

"Okay," a voice said and the door opened.

Casey went in. Another man in a dinner jacket was waiting, an older fellow with a bony face and bags under his eyes.

"He hasn't got a card," the youth said.

"Hello, Nick." Casey shrugged out of his coat, handed it and his hat to the statuesque blonde that was coming toward him from the room opposite the stairs.

"Why don't you carry your card?" Nick said.

"I never had one," Casey said. "What's the beef? You know me."

"Tony doesn't." Nick looked at the hard-eyed youth.

"Tony does now," Casey said. "Don't you, Tony?"

The youth cursed him with his lips, making no sound. Nick walked with Casey to the stairs.

"Feeling lucky tonight?"

"No," said Casey. "Thirsty."

He glanced into the deserted living-room with the floor lamp for a decoy, climbed silently on the stair carpet. A squarish, softly lighted room opened off the second-floor landing and Casey went into a luxuriously furnished lounge with a bar at one side and a lot of mirrors and oversized prints scattered about. There were two men at the bar; three women and two other men standing near one corner, glasses in their hands. The men were in evening clothes, the women in dinner gowns. They wasted only a glance at Casey and went on talking.

One of the men at the bar came toward him. "Hello, Flash," he said. "Get yourself a drink. How you going?"

"On the beam," Casey said. "Bernie, Dixon around?"

"Telephoning, I think. Yes— There he is now." Casey saw Dixon come out of the telephone booth and waited until he came up.

"Looking for me, Casey?" he asked.

"How'd you know?"

"Dominic called and told me. How about a drink?"

Casey said all right and they went to the bar, leaving the third man behind—Alec Thomas, his name was. He ran the place.

The bartender took their orders and Dixon said nothing more until his drink was placed before him.

"Luck," he said, and drank. "Anything important?"

"No." Casey turned and put his back to the bar. "I was looking for Perry Austin. He was going to your place to get some pictures."

"He did."

Casey sipped his drink. "How was the contest?"

"Great. Only they had me on the air from twelve to twelve-thirty introducing people and making speeches. You should've dropped in."

Casey studied Dixon carefully over his glass. He was a lithe, wiry man of 35 or so, with thinning brown hair, which he wore parted in the middle and plastered back, and small, deep-set eyes that were as opaque and fathomless as well water. The dinner jacket he wore must have cost a $150 and looked it. His collar and tie were immaculate, he wore a platinum wrist watch, and on his little finger was a platinum ring set with a star sapphire. His trousers had lots of pleats and a fine gold chain was looped from his pocket. The only thing wrong was the aggregate effect—he was too smooth, too immaculate, too studied.

"I wish I could have," Casey said. "Only I got hooked up in that Endicott murder."

Nothing moved in Dixon's face. He was examining his highball glass, turning it as he did so. "I heard about it. What happened?"

"He was stretched out on the floor when I got there."

"When you got there?"

"Me and Austin."

"Oh." It was just a word with no inflection. He was still inspecting his glass. "He was a nice guy, Stan. It's a hard one to figure."

Casey waited, watching covertly. Dixon took some more of his drink. "Has the law got any angles yet?"

"They think maybe he was killed before he could talk."

"About what? That bond rap?"

"Um-hum. They think he wasn't the only one in it and maybe knew too much. They think maybe the guy that did it beat it down the back stairs and got away in a small sedan."

"That's a good start," Dixon said. He' said other things too, but Casey replied automatically because he was thinking about Dixon and not what he said. What his racket had been in New York, Casey did not know. In fact no one had paid much attention to him until he started the Club Berkely four or five years ago. Now everything was changed. The Berkely was *the* place—and apparently it had netted Bernie Dixon a fortune. People made a fuss over him these days, and fought for ringside tables and the publicity attendant upon their getting them. He catered to personalities of all kinds.

Yet there had never been any unpleasant publicity connected with the establishment. Nothing rowdy was tolerated and what few fights occurred there were of the one-punch variety peculiar to the breed of nightclub cavaliers. Casey remembered all these things and more. He remembered what Logan had said about Dixon and Mrs. Endicott, that Dixon had been a client of Endicott. And all of a sudden Casey was wondering whether this was the man he had seen behind the wheel of the little sedan when he had taken that picture.

He realized Dixon had become silent and said, "When did Austin leave?"

"I didn't see him. He was there earlier. Around ten-thirty, I know, because he took some pictures. After that I was too busy to notice. We had five girls in the finals. They all had to do a turn—you know, sing or dance or something."

"Was he there when you got there?"

"I think he was."

"And when was that?"

"About ten o'clock."

"Oh. You got there at ten."

"Yes."

Casey hadn't realized he, was staring until he caught the inflection of that word; now he saw that the man was watching him, his little eyes half-hidden, his smile tight and mirthless. He put down his glass. He looked up at Casey with those prying, fathomless eyes and his voice was clipped but measured.

"Yes, I got there about ten, Casey." He turned away, stopped to say, "Why don't you stop in some time? I'll see that you get a good table."

Casey swung back to the bar and ordered another drink. When it was put down in front of him he drank slowly and stared with troubled eyes at the row of bottles on the opposite counter. He still wondered about Austin, although he was not much worried since he did not believe the picture of the sedan would turn out to be of any value. He was much more worried about Finell, and the picture of Lyda Hoyt that had been stolen from his desk. It made him so discouraged thinking about it that in the end he gulped his drink and turned away, heading for the telephone.

Bernie Dixon was just crossing the room from the direction of the booth. He did not appear to see Casey, but continued to the stairs to the gambling-room above. Casey watched him go before he asked for the hospital.

Wade opened up the moment he heard Casey's voice. "Listen," he protested. "Do I have to sit here all night?"

"Has Finell come to yet?"

"No. And if I don't get a drink I'm going to crawl in with him."

"All right," Casey said. "We'll call it off for tonight."

"What about the drink?"

"Quit crabbin' and I'll buy you one."

"Yes, you will," Wade scoffed. "At this hour?"

"Yes, at this hour," Casey said and gave him the address of the house. "Grab yourself a cab and come on out. And listen, if they stop you at the door just ask for Nick and mention my name."

He hung up and stood for a moment fighting off the pressure of weariness and dejection before he opened the door and stepped out. As he turned he bumped into a man and would have knocked him down had he not grabbed him in time. Then he saw who it was.

"Flash Casey." A slender, angular fellow with rimless glasses and rumpled blond hair was grinning at him. His name was McCann and he was a free-lance, publicity man. Right now he was pretty drunk, but the most startling thing about him was the sheaf of money in his hand. "Ol' Flash, ol' boy, ol' boy."

"Hi, Mac," Casey said.

McCann patted him on the shoulder with a limp, double-action movement of his wrist. "Take a look," he said and waved the bills under Casey's nose. "Smell it. Brother, am I hot."

"Damned if you're not," said Casey.

"Count it." McCann slapped the bills into Casey's palm. "Go ahead. Tell me how hot I am."

Casey took the money. There was a $20 and a $10 and 12 new $50's. "Six hundred and thirty bucks."

"We'll double it." McCann gave him that double-action wrist again and took his arm. "Come on. Up we go."

"Wait a minute." Casey pulled him to a stop. "Let's go home and celebrate," he said. "We'll get a cab."

McCann gave him a sly leer. He shook his finger. "No, you don't."

Casey grinned in spite of himself. No one was dumber than a foxy drunk. He'd been that way himself, spending hours trying to outsmart himself just as McCann was going to do. "Get smart," he said, making a last attempt. "You got yours, get out. Go back upstairs and you'll drop the works."

"Who cares?" McCann said. "I like to see that little ball go round'n'round."

Casey sighed and took his arm. In his condition McCann would never get out of the place with that money, but Casey made up his mind to see that he lost it legitimately.

They went to the rear of the room and opened a door and climbed the stairs; then they were in a narrow hall that had two abrupt angles in it, at the edge of which were sliding steel doors, now retracted. Beyond was a low-ceilinged room, smoke-filled, softly, lighted, and quiet. At the far end was a cashier's window; on either side were crap tables and in the center two roulette layouts. Only one was operating now and there were but five players, four men, one of them Dixon, and a woman.

One of the men looked up as Casey and McCann approached; the others were intent upon the wheel. No word was spoken as McCann tossed down two fifty-dollar bills. The croupier automatically stuffed them in a slot in the table and slid some chips to one side.

The ball came to a stop and he raked in the bets. Pausing a moment as new bets were placed, he spun it again. McCann put a quarter of his chips on 17. The woman looked at him. She was a bleached blonde of 50 or so with a diamond choker and a half-pound of diamonds on her two hands.

Casey lit a cigarette and watched McCann lose his $100 in four spins. He got more chips, cut down the size of his bets but made more of them; playing the 0 and the block around 17. He won twice but within five minutes the second $100 was gone. Casey took his arm. "Come here," he said and dragged him to one side.

McCann gave him a drunken grin. "How'm I doin'?"

"Terrific," said Casey. "Look." He lowered his voice and pulled McCann closer. "Can you let me have a couple of yards?"

"Sure. You wanna play?"

"No. I—"

McCann looked up at him, the foxiness in his eyes again. "No, you don't," he said, wagging his finger. "I know you. You can't—"

"But listen." Casey turned on the sadness. "I mean it. I'm behind on the payments on my car. I got a notice today. And the last install-ment on my income tax is due. I'm in a spot, kid."

McCann weakened. "Now wait a minute—"

"If you can't make it two, make it a yard and a half."

"Aw, here." McCann wiped three 50's from the thin stack. "Here. Stop makin' me cry."

Casey watched him stagger back to the table and then he saw that the croupier's assistant was watching him. The fellow was a jut-jawed husky and he knew what had happened and he didn't like it. He didn't know how much Casey had nicked McCann for, but he did know that whatever it was, the house wouldn't get it that night. He bunched his lips and glowered.

At the doorway he turned. The man was still glowering. Casey waved at him. He felt pretty good going downstairs, thinking how he'd saved something out for McCann, and then he thought about Wade and glanced at his strap watch.

It was well after two now and be turned toward the bar, mum-bling to himself, determined to have one more drink and then go home to bed whether Wade came or not. He got the drink and drank it, neither hurrying nor taking his time; when Wade did not appear he went downstairs, bought his coat and hat back from the blonde, and went out with a good night for Nick and a chuckle for the youth with patent-leather hair who accompanied him to the outer door.

"You ought to watch yourself." Casey said. "You hadn't ought to let people in here unless they show their card."

The youth cursed as the door closed behind Casey. He buttoned his coat, standing on the top step and glancing up and down the street. When he couldn't *see* Wade, he went down the steps toward his car.

There was a man sitting on the bottom step of the house next door. He was smoking a cigarette:

"See you a minute?" he said hoarsely.

Casey paused. The man stood up. "You're Casey, ain't yuh?" he said. And then, before Casey could answer, he saw the gun and stiffened, hearing a sound of movement behind him, half-turning toward it as a second man walked from between two parked cars.

"Stand still!" the first man said. The other stepped up behind Casey and jabbed a gun in his back. The first man circled round so that he, too, was behind Casey and slightly to one side. "'Down the street, pal," he said. "We'll tell you when to stop."

Casey hesitated but a moment. If he'd had any chance to give them an argument it was gone now and he knew it. He started along the sidewalk.

CHAPTER EIGHT
AN OLD-FASHIONED RIDE

CASEY DID A LOT OF THINKING as he walked slowly along that darkened street. The first startled thought that had come to him at the sight of the gun was that he was being stuck up; then he remembered something and knew that there was more behind the attempt than that.

The man on the steps had asked his name. He had been waiting—not for just any victim but for Casey. And the way the other fellow had waited out of sight between the two parked cars, ready for any move that Casey might make, proved that these two were not amateurs. They had a special job to do, and thinking about it brought the perspiration out on Casey's brow.

They made him walk past two parked cars and stop opposite a third. It was a dark sedan, a three-year-old model. One of the men opened the rear door and the other said, "Get in, friend."

The gun jabbed hard against his spine and was removed as he took a forward step. He stopped. A car raced by on the other side of the street, a girl's laughter drifting across to him from a lowered window. He looked up and down the pavement. Blocks away he saw the headlights of another car coming toward him. He turned slowly.

The two men were waiting, not close where he might make a pass at them, but a good four feet away, side by side, guns barely visible and hip high. He had never seen either of them before and wondered about it, noting now that they were about the same size, neither tall nor short, one—the one who had first spoken to him—somewhat thinner than his companion. Both wore dark, tight-fitting coats with the collars snapped up and folded across their throats. The thin man wore a dark felt; his companion had a light-gray one with a narrow band.

"In," the thin man said. "Or do we have to lay you out here?" said the other.

Casey backed up a step, measuring them, feeling the stiffness in his muscles. The headlights of the car he had noticed down the street swept by, outlining the three of them briefly. Down the block a manhole cover banged hollowly as the car sped over it; then the darkness came again and nothing had changed. He felt his way into the back of the car.

"Now down, pal," the thin man said. "On your knees."

"Nuts," said Casey.

"'Nuts,' he says," said the one with the gray hat. "If he moves a whisker let him have it," he said, and walked around the car. He opened the rear door, leaned in and cocked his wrist. Casey thought he could duck away from the blow that was coming, but he still had one eye on the other man's gun and didn't dare.

"Okay," he said and slid off the seat.

"You see?" Gray Hat said. "What do you have to argue for?"

Casey was on his knees now, wedged in between the back of the front seat and the cushion of the rear one. The thin man got in and sat down in the opposite corner, slamming the door; his partner climbed in behind the wheel.

From his spot on the floor Casey couldn't see much of the

outside scenery—tops of trees and the upper stories of houses and apartments at first and then, after a few turns, sections of stores and office buildings. The thin man had pulled down the rear curtain soon after they started and remained hunched far back in the corner, his short-barreled revolver resting on his knee and slanting at Casey.

They were moving moderately fast with no traffic lights to bother them and presently Casey's knees began to get sore. There were some long, rounded objects under him that felt like rollers and no matter how he shifted his weight he could not seem to get away from them.

He watched the thin man. He could see him more distinctly now, and as the car whipped past street lamps, reflected segments of their rays would flick through the tonneau, highlighting briefly the fellow's face. It looked smooth and sallow and tightly drawn across the cheekbones. The nose was flattened across the nostrils but narrowed sharply and where the bridge should have been was a sharp depression, as though someone had chiseled out a piece of the bone.

"Where the hell are we going?" he said finally.

"Gettin' anxious?" the man asked flatly.

"I'm getting damned uncomfortable."

"We'll fix that for. you," the man said, and Casey didn't like the way he said it.

He looked at the rear curtain, wondering about its translucence and the light behind it. He studied it absently for a minute or so without getting any answer, or caring much. They turned a corner. The light beyond the curtain seemed to fall away and then, seconds later, became again more noticeable.

Quick hope plucked sharply at his taut nerves. A car? Could that light he saw be headlights? He tried to swallow and found his throat dry. He stared at the curtain, yellowish now because of what was behind it. Then, as the hope began to build and his pulse quickened, the car swerved sharply and the light faded and no longer was the pavement smooth beneath him, but bumpy and uneven.

Casey let his breath out and something inside him seemed to collapse and the weariness and dejection was on him again. There wasn't any light behind them now. The car was slowing down. His knees were getting sore from the pounding of the rough pavement and he put his hands down to see if he could get those rollers out from under him. Suddenly it seemed cooler and the breeze that came through the lowered front window was fresher, somehow, and moist.

Casey got hold of a roller and the instant he touched it he froze and his breath caught in his throat. He knew what the score was now. He knew why they hadn't shot him back on the Avenue when he started to get stubborn, knew why the air sweeping through the window felt fresh and moist. He could smell it now. Salt and eel grass and marshes.

The thing—that roller he had his hand on—was a sash weight!

Something clammy crawled into his brain and coiled there. He could feel his scalp prickle. He slid his fingers along the sash weight. A big one—seven or eight pounds; there were a half-dozen of them, or more. There'd be rope, too. He could not feel it but he knew it would be there.

The car had almost stopped. The thin man leaned forward on the seat. It was dark inside the tonneau now and Casey slid his hand along the floor in front of him, carefully, groping for a weight that he could get his fingers on, that was not pinned beneath him. He found one finally and knew what he had to do.

This was a good old-fashioned ride. He had photographed such victims many times in the old prohibition days. These men had a similar job to do and their orders had been to put him away where he would not be found. A couple of slugs in the head and 50 or 60 pounds of iron on his ankles. What better way than that? By the time the ropes—or his ankles—rotted away nobody would ever identify him.

All right. If that's the way it was, it was the chance and not the odds that counted, and suddenly he found that he was no longer panicky and uncertain, but poised and confident and alert. Even his brain was cool and clear, now that he knew what he had to do; he even had time for a curious sardonic digression as he thought: *If I muff this, old McCann is going to be out a 150 bucks. Boy, will he be sore*— He slid his fingers along the sash weight and waited, muscles tensing.

The car stopped. "This is it," he said. But he didn't swing the sash weight. He never even picked it up. Because just then something slammed him against the back of the front seat and there was a terrific crash of sound and he thought a gun had gone off, that he had been hit.

What he did then was pure reflex. He still didn't know what had happened. He may have been a little stunned by the suddenness of it but he wasted no time asking himself questions. Wedged against the cushion, he had felt the jar but kept his balance. That evened up the odds, which was all Casey ever asked.

The thin man, knocked off the seat by the impact, was struggling on the floor and Casey forgot the sash weight and pounced on him, groping for the gun. Not until then did he see that both rear doors had been knocked open; that told him that another car had crashed into the back of the sedan and by that time he had found the man's wrist and jerked the gun free.

Still on his knees, he chopped with it twice, slapping it against the corner of a jaw and then bringing it down on the black felt hat. He swiveled, trying to swing at the man behind the wheel, but the other saw the blow coming and ducked and slid out from behind the wheel, stumbling as he hit the ground. Casey bucked backward through the open door. He wasn't thinking much about himself then, because all the pent-up emotions that had been building inside him for the past few minutes broke violently, leaving anger and resentment a blind and driving force.

There was perhaps one instant when the man in front could have used his gun. That he did not may have been due to his befuddled condition; it may have been that he saw the gun in Casey's hand and was afraid. Whatever the reason, he spun and fled into the shadows and Casey chased him, yelling at him to, stop.

They ran past the car behind the sedan, a curiously familiar car to Casey, and then the man fired over his shoulder without slowing down and Casey stopped and squeezed the trigger, aiming low. The gun slapped back against the heel of his hand in recoil and the vague figure in front of him went down on his face as though his legs had been cut from under him.

Casey heard the gun skid across the cobblestones and walked slowly toward it. He groped for it, put it in his coat pocket. He went back to the prostrate gunman and prodded him with his toe. The fellow began to writhe upon the ground. "Get up!" Casey said.

"Oh, God!" the fellow whined. "I can't."

Casey glanced back at the two cars. The door of the convertible was opening and he knew now why it had seemed familiar. It was his. And that would be that crazy Wade getting out.

"Watch the guy in the sedan," he called; then prodded the gunman again. "You got a bum leg, so what? I should've let you have it in the back."

He reached down and stood the man on his feet.

"You're the ones that slugged Finell, huh? And stole my plate, case."

The other remained mute and limped along as Casey pulled him toward the sedan. Wade was peering into the tonneau.

"How is he?" Casey asked.

"Tired," Wade said.

"Drag him out."

He looked past the sedan where the headlights cut into the blackness. Just beyond was a ramshackle building and a broken-down wharf. He wasn't sure just where he was but he could see the decayed piles and the string pieces at the end. Beyond was nothing but blackness and water. He shivered and looked away.

Wade had the thin man on his feet and Casey made the two of them walk down in front of the sedan and stand in its headlights, their hands up.

"Where the hell were you?" he said to Wade, gruffly because his nerves hadn't quite settled down. "Why didn't you come to the club?"

"Where was I?" Wade was indignant. "Out in the cold, you cluck. They wouldn't let me in. Just mention my name, you said. That's all. Just mention it. Go ahead. I dare you. You know what happens when you mention your name? They try to bounce you down the stairs."

"Who did?"

"That tough little monkey in the vestibule with the patent-leather hair."

Casey almost grinned then. "So you waited out in my car?"

"Where else?"

Casey had backed up a step so he could look at the front end of his car. The bumper was twisted and bent but the fenders looked all right.

"And you saw them grab me and followed us," he said. "I thought there was a car behind us, but when we turned down here—"

"The lights went off," Wade finished. "I turned 'em off. When

I started I thought we might scare up a radio car but we didn't and I had to keep going. Then when I saw you were going to turn off, I got scared."

"*You* got scared?"

"I switched off my lights and tailed you down. I didn't know what would happen but when I saw the water and the car stop I knew I had to give you a chance."

"You did all right," Casey said. "You did swell. The only thing wrong is that things like this have to happen when I haven't got a camera."

"That's Casey for you," Wade said. "He never gets the breaks." He began to whistle softly and Casey scowled across the darkness, trying to see what he was doing. Wade opened the door of the convertible and leaned in. When he reappeared he had a plate case in his hand. "Ho hum," he said. "You know this could make page one."

Casey just gaped at him. He watched Wade take out the camera and screw in a flash bulb. Finally he found his voice.

"Where'd you get it?"

"I had it," Wade said. "I took it to the hospital with me. I brought it along in the cab. I used it for a pillow in your car— You think these are the two lugs that slugged Finell?"

Casey shook his head and walked toward the front of the sedan. *That Wade,* he thought. *What a guy.* He looked at the two gunmen. They had their hands down now but he didn't care. The wounded one was standing on one leg and leaning on his partner.

"Hurry up," Casey said. "Grab a couple and then take my car and find a phone. Call Logan."

"And just mention your name, huh?"

Casey sat down on the bumper. He couldn't think of anything to say. He just waited there watching Wade take his pictures.

CHAPTER NINE

GOOD-BY, MR. GARRISON

CASEY WAS TIRED. He knew he should get up, but he did not want to, and stretched under the covers and turned over to catch a little more sleep. He closed his eyes, but by that time the events of the night before had begun to flow through his mind. That made him start to think, and once he started, he opened his eyes again.

He could see, in imagination, the two thugs. He remembered vividly the ride, the sash weights on the floor of the tonneau, the blackness of the water beyond the abandoned wharf. Then Tom Wade driving the convertible into the back of the sedan to give him a chance to fight for it.

By now he was pretty sure what had happened. Someone had sent the two men to watch Stanford Endicott's apartment after the murder. That someone was the man Casey had followed down the back stairs, the man who had been in the sedan when Casey snapped the picture. Whoever it was, he could not be certain how that picture would turn out. He had to have it. He had sent the two gunmen, and when Casey had come out with Lieutenant Logan and Sergeant Manahan, the two had followed the police car to Endicott's apartment. While Casey was with the police questioning Mrs. Endicott, the plate case had been stolen.

It would take the gunmen some time to find out what was on the exposed film in that plate case and when the picture they wanted was not there, they had come to the *Express* building in search of it. Somehow they had run into Finell, slugged him, jimmied Casey's desk. They hadn't found the picture they sought but had seen the shot of Lyda Hoyt—

Casey sat up, a thrust of apprehension freezing his thoughts. He swung his feet to the floor, reached down beside the telephone box, pulled it off, and slipped out the piece of felt which was his silencer when he wanted to be sure his sleep would not be interrupted. He put the cover back, swept the instrument from the table, and gave the operator the number of police headquarters.

A nerve jumped in his jaw as he waited. There was no longer any sleep in the corners of his eyes but only darkness and worry. He'd forgotten about that picture when he left Logan the night before. Suppose one of the gunmen had it on him? Suppose Logan had it now?

"Hello," he said. "What did you—"

"Where the hell've you been?" Logan said curtly. "I tried to get you an hour ago."

"The phone's been out of order," Casey said. "What about those two punks? Did they sing for you?"

"They didn't have to. There's fugitive warrants out on both of them. Maybe we ought to give you a merit badge."

"Nuts," said Casey. "Who are they?"

"A couple of guns from Jersey. They're hooked up in the Murder Syndicate, remember?"

Casey remembered. The case had broken about six months previous and the papers had been full of the fantastic details of the so-called organization whose business was murder for profit. Two or three of the mob had already been convicted, some were awaiting trial, others were being hunted down.

"But what were they doing here?" he asked finally. "I mean how did they—"

"That's what we're going to find out."

Casey waited. Logan went on to give some more details and Casey knew then that the picture had not been found; otherwise he'd be hearing about it now. He lay back on the bed, breathing a little easier as Logan continued.

"It's like I told you," he said. "You always fall into the breaks. You saw the guy run out of Endicott's apartment. You didn't recognize him—" Logan's voice grew thin and remote. "You say you didn't, anyway."

"I didn't."

"All right. But he recognized you. He gave those two rats a job to do and they'd have done it, if it hadn't been for Wade— So watch yourself. You'd better stop in on your way down."

Casey put the telephone away, slipped out of his pajama coat and let the trousers fall. He went over and closed the window, stretched, and ran his fingers through his tousled hair. He stood a moment, breathing deeply, a powerful-looking figure, solidly muscled, his stomach hard and flat; then he went into the bath and turned on the shower.

He had finished shaving and was putting on his tie when the buzzer sounded. Waiting long enough to run a comb through his hair, he left the bedroom and crossed the living-room. He snapped back the bolt and opened the door.

Nat Garrison stood in the hall. Casey saw that much in the first general glimpse; after that his gaze centered on the muzzle of the gun in Garrison's hand.

"Back up."

Casey's nerves began to stretch but he pretended he didn't see the gun. He put on what he thought was a grin and made his voice indulgent. "Oh, hello, Nat. Come in."

He turned his back on the man and walked to the center of the room. There was an enameled cigarette box on the table. He picked it up, hearing the door close behind him. He selected a cigarette and turned to offer the box. Garrison watched him narrowly, saying nothing. After that Casey had to notice the gun. He acted surprised as though he'd just seen it.

"Hey. What's this? Put that thing away, will you? I haven't had breakfast yet."

"They're lookin' for me." Garrison's lips didn't move when he spoke and his eyes were ugly. "You told 'em."

"Wait a minute." Casey lit the cigarette and sat down. "Told who what?" he stalled.

"You saw me come out of Endicott's building last night. I didn't think you pegged me but you did. You squawked. Every flattie in town is lookin' for me."

Casey didn't say anything, but studied the man a moment through the smoke screen he blew out. About average height, stocky, but not so solid-looking anymore. Like most fighters he had put on weight when he left the ring; he had put on more weight in prison. "All right," he said bluntly. "They're looking for you. What do you want?"

Garrison blinked, as though he hadn't expected the question and wasn't ready for it. "I didn't knock off Endicott," he said.

"All right. You didn't knock him off"

"He was alive when I left."

"Okay."

"He had some dough of mine. Five G's. He was holding it for me while I did my stretch." Garrison twitched his shoulder and rubbed the back of his hand across his nose. "He was out of town when I came out. So last night I went up there. He told me he didn't have the cash, that he'd get it today."

"What do you want?"

Garrison's eyes grew more obscure. The heavy automatic moved in his hand. "You ain't goin' around sayin' you saw me come out of that building."

Casey put out his cigarette and waited.

"All I got to do is squeeze this thing a couple times," Garrison said, moving the gun again.

"Sure." Casey rose, carefully, unhurriedly. "So then they burn you for it."

"Un-unh. Nobody saw me come up here. Nobody's gonna see me leave. I'm not gonna get framed for that Endicott thing. With you out of the way I can go down and take my beating from those headquarters bastards, but that's all. Nobody's gonna be around to put the finger on me."

Casey looked at him. It was pretty hard to believe, but recalling other things, he felt a growing stiffness come over him and the faint tightening of his scalp. The guy was crazy. Yeah. That was the trouble. He'd been a pretty fair middleweight. He'd fought for the title once, but he'd always been a puncher, an iron man, and like all the rest he had taken a terrific pounding because of that. Even after he'd been knocked out a couple of times, he'd gone on thinking his defeats had been flukes and that he was better than he ever was.

Thinking of these things, seeing the mean mouth and the glassy narrowness of the man's eyes, Casey began to sweat. He still couldn't believe the fellow would shoot, and yet he could not predict the course of safety. He took a chance at pretending the whole thing was ridiculous.

"You've been hittin' the weed again," he jeered.

"Who?"

"You. Beat it, will you? I haven't had breakfast."

"You think I'm kiddin'?" Garrison took a slow forward step. "You think I ain't got what it takes to make this talk?"

"Sure you have. But you got good sense too. If you could do it and get away, sure. But you can't. Not here. You can beat the Endicott thing but you couldn't beat this, Nat."

He turned away as he spoke, turned back slowly as Garrison snapped, "Stand still, damn you!"

Casey took pains with his words. "I got to make a phone call."

"No, you don't."

"I have to call the office and tell them not to run the story."

"What story?"

"The one I turned in about you." Casey shrugged. He was still sweating but his voice was right. "I thought I'd give you a break and kill it. Of course if you don't care—" He broke off, shrugging.

Garrison squinted at him, suspicion filming his gaze. You could practically see his brain struggling. Finally he nodded. "Go ahead. I'll go with you."

Casey went into the bedroom. He picked up the telephone, watching Garrison stop at the door. He gave the number of the *Express* and when he was connected he asked for the desk, leaning back against the wall as he waited, reaching down with his right hand, shielding his hand with his body as he felt for a corner of the pillow. There were two of these and the one on this side was so close that he did not have to lean down to touch it. He got his hand on the corner as Bennett, the day man, answered.

"Casey. Yeah. You know that story on Nat Garrison?" He could bear Bennett asking what the hell he was talking about, but he winked at Garrison and went right ahead. "Well, Nat's here in my place now. He's got a gun on me and I wanted to tell you, so if I get knocked off this morning you'll be sure he burns for it."

He held the telephone, hearing Bennett yelling at him. He kept grinning, watching only Garrison's gun hand, the pressure of the finger on the trigger. He started to hang up, still holding to the pillow, every muscle tensed so that he could throw it and duck if he had to.

For an interminable second he watched the gun; then his glance struck at the man's face and he saw the confusion and puzzlement there and knew somehow, that it was all right, that the crisis was past. He kept grinning, putting the telephone aside but making no other move. Finally Garrison added it all up.

"Why, you—" he snarled. "Why, you bastard! You double-crossing bastard!" His scarred face twisted and untwisted and his hand moved on the gun but his trigger finger did not tighten.

"You see?" Casey blew out his breath. He let go of the pillow. "It was a bad idea, Nat. Nobody's going to frame you for anything. I had to make sure you I wouldn't blaze away and burn for it."

Garrison backed into the living-room. "All right," he fumed. "But don't think it makes any difference. This morning. Tonight. What do I care. I got time. Those cops ain't gonna pick me up for a while." He was at the door now, feeling behind him to open it, still clinging to the gun. "Tell the cops you made a mistake and have it in this afternoon's paper or else."

Casey watched the door slam. He got out his handkerchief and mopped his face. He still didn't know whether Garrison had really intended to shoot or whether he'd come to throw a bluff; all he knew was that for a couple of minutes he'd been scared as hell.

Back in the bedroom, he called Bennett again and explained what had happened. Then he got his coat and hat and went down to the corner restaurant where he found he had an appetite and ate fruit and cereal, boiled eggs, muffins, and coffee. When he came out he felt a little better physically but this was offset by his sultry mood.

Ever since he'd started in Endicott's office he'd been pushed around—by the police and Blaine and the two gunmen and Nat Garrison and Grant Forrester. It wouldn't have seemed so bad if he had a few answers, if he was sure of the reason why all this was happening. That was the trouble. He had some hunches, nothing more, and as his thoughts flowed on he remembered something else and swung the convertible left at the next corner.

A three- or four-minute ride brought him to a solid row of brownstone fronts that, while old, managed to maintain a certain air of neatness and respectability.

Casey started to slow down in the middle of the block, and then he saw that by angling its nose to the curb and letting the rear stick put in the street, a taxi had hogged the space in front of the house he sought.

"Why don't you park double?" he growled.

The driver turned irritably on the seat but the crack he was about to make was left unsaid when he saw Casey. The irritation dissolved in a grin.

"Hyuh, Flash Gun. If I'd a known you was comin' I'd a run her up on the sidewalk."

Casey went on by and wrenched the convertible into a parking-space. "You oughta be ashamed, Augie," he said when he came back, but there was no sting in his admonishment.

"Sorry, pal," Augie said. "I'm waitin' for a fare."

Casey saw then that the cab's motor was running, and thought no more about it as he climbed the stone steps and walked through the open door to the vestibule. He went up the stairs along the wall as he had done the night before, turned right at the landing, and knocked at the door on the left, his thoughts returning once more to the grudge he had against the world.

Even Perry Austin had crossed him up the night before, not showing up with that film holder he was supposed to take to the office. He knocked again as he wondered if the fellow had returned to the *Express* after he, Casey, had gone in search of Bernie Dixon. In any event it did not look as if Austin was home this time either. He tried the door. It was unlocked.

He went in, through an entryway to the living-room that over-looked the street and smelled of staleness and cigarette smoke. Perry was here all right, and seeing him, Casey stopped cold and a sudden vacuum hit him in the pit of the stomach. For Austin lay on the floor.

He looked as if he had been there a long time. Except for the dinner jacket and the bloodstained shirt front, he looked almost like Stanford Endicott had looked the night before.

CHAPTER TEN

COMPANY FOR THE CORPSE

CASEY STOOD THERE QUITE A WHILE until he remembered he had left the door open. By that time he felt he could move and went back and closed it. He returned to the living-room, glancing down at the body but not moving up to inspect it, and sat down in the nearest chair, feeling all weak and sick inside.

It was not the sight of death, as such, that brought the sickness, nor the fact that Austin, though not his friend, had worked beside him for two years; this alone was enough to sadden and dishearten him, but it was the frightful and inescapable explanation of the scene that left him crushed and defenseless before all that bitterness and nausea.

Perry Austin was dead and he, Casey, was responsible. He had taken a picture of the killer fleeing from Stanford Endicott's offices. He had given that picture to Austin. Somehow the killer had found out about it and Austin had been killed because of it. There was no other answer. That had to be it.

He stirred in his chair, his broad face slack and miserable and despondent. Unable to shake aside that awful feeling of guilt, he forced his glance slowly about the room. There was a plate case on the floor near one wall but Casey was so convinced of his solution that he could not bring himself to inspect it. The film holder he had given Austin would not be there. It would not be in his Chesterfield which lay across a chair back on the opposite side of the room.

In one corner was a kneehole desk. He could see from here that the middle drawer was part-way open. The film holder would not be in the desk either. That film holder was gone— He made himself get up and move to the body. He put the back of his hand to the blue-white cheek. It was stone cold. He picked up a wrist and found the arm stiff and inflexible.

"A long time," he said bitterly. "Last night. That's why I couldn't find him." He recalled his trip here. When was that? A little after 12:00. Had Austin been here then, or had he come back to meet his death at some later hour?

Casey did not know and realized that speculation did no good. There were a lot of whys and wherefores vortexing through his brain but no escaping the conclusion. He looked down at the body again. There was a lot of blood on the rug, dried now and making an ugly stain. There was a gun too, a foot or so to one side of the right hand. A .32 Colt Automatic.

Casey wondered if this was the same gun that had killed Endicott but he did not touch it. He unbuttoned the dinner jacket and lifted it back. There were two holes in that starched shirt front. He straightened, eyes going back to the plate case. He took a step toward it, felt something under his heel and stepped aside to look down and see what it was.

An empty shell. When he picked it up he saw that his weight had made an ellipse of the former roundness and left a sharp outline in the rug. Knowing there'd be another somewhere around, but not bothering to look for it, he tossed it on the desk and continued to the plate case.

It was closed but unfastened and he opened it. There were three film holders which had never been exposed but none that had been used. He went to the coat on the chair and slapped the pockets, knowing now that his original conviction had been right. There would be no exposed film holders. Whoever had murdered Austin had taken them all to make sure.

Habit was strong in Casey and without realizing it he took Austin's camera from the plate case, inserted a film holder and screwed a flash bulb into the synchronized gun. He checked the shutter speed and aperture, walking around the body as he did so, his photographer's eye searching for the best angle. When he had his picture he reversed the film holder, tossed the used bulb into the plate case and selected a fresh one. For this part was still a job, and pictures had to be taken when the opportunity presented itself, regardless of what went on inside you.

He felt for a cigarette as he visualized his next shot, lit it, and dropped the match in an ash tray on the table. That he saw the cigarette butt at all was one of those things that make subsequent explanation difficult. In spite of his preoccupation, in spite of the fact that he gave it but a passing glance, something about that cigarette butt rang a gong inside his head and, frowning, he looked again and picked it up.

It was about half-consumed and much bent from being crushed out. He held it at the bend, seeing the stain of red where lips had held it, seeing something more. He touched the stain lightly, then pressed it between thumb and finger. That told him what he had suspected when he first saw it. This butt was fresh; the end was still damp.

His eyes came up and began to circle the room while a tightness grew in his chest. He was looking for hiding-places now, not knowing whether the woman who had left the lipstick on that cigarette was still here or not. But there was no place of concealment in this room and the only doorway, other than the one through which he had entered, opened to an inner hall almost directly ahead.'

The tightness was still with him as he moved silently forward. He had smelled smoke when he entered, but it had seemed stale then and now he knew it wasn't. Somehow he had the feeling that the smoker was still in the apartment and, moving into the hall and seeing the closed door there, he decided he was about to get a few answers.

He took his time about it, seeing the open doorway leading to a bedroom, another doorway, and the kitchen beyond. He glanced into the bedroom but did not leave the hall. He looked into the kitchen. He came back to the closed door, deciding it was a closet, that if he was in a hurry to hide he might pick it as a likely place.

"Come on out!" he said abruptly, and reached for the knob. He yanked the door toward him, the camera still in his left hand. And then, drawn back against the coats that hung there, he saw her—the girl who had come to the studio looking for Perry Austin the evening before.

She wore a loose coat, a hat of dark green felt. Her face was white and set and that made her lipsticked mouth look scarlet; her eyes were wide and startled, but in their hazel depths was determination rather than fear. Under her left arm was an oversized handbag. In her right fist was a tiny automatic.

For a long moment the tight hard silence held them mute and immobile. She let her breath out slowly, waited, then caught it sharply. The silence fled and Casey's mouth tightened into a thin, hard line. He looked at the gun, let his narrowed stare come back to hers, and found it steady and defiant.

"Hello," he said finally. "Remember me?"

Something flickered in the hazel eyes and died away. Her voice came cold and distant. "Please step away from that door!"

Casey sized her up again, measuring the gun, not knowing what this was all about but deciding not to grab for it. He grinned crookedly and backed slowly into the living-room. "All right," he said. "You finally found him, didn't you?"

She followed silently, circling as he stood there, avoiding the symbol of death on the floor but not looking at it.

"What did you want with him last night? When I met you out in the hall you said he wasn't in."

"He wasn't."

"He's been dead quite a while." He was moving slowly toward the door as he spoke, trying to work closer and cut her off. Suddenly she saw what he was doing and stopped.

"Stand right where you are, please."

Casey took another slow step, his eyes smoldering, speculative.

"I'm not afraid to shoot."

He stopped, seeing her hand tighten on the gun. He didn't know whether to believe her or not. He had no ideas about whether she had killed Perry Austin. He did not think she had, although this thought had no solid basis in fact. He did want to know who she was and what she knew. "Did you kill him?" he asked.

She caught her breath. "No. No, of course I didn't. I don't know anything about it. I just—"

"Then you'd be sort of silly, wouldn't you? Starting in on me?"

"I wouldn't kill you." He saw her jaw set, the tightening of her mouth. "I'd—just shoot you in the leg."

"Yeah, you might at that," Casey said, and suddenly he knew what he was going to do.

She took another tentative step. He made no move and she took another. He held the camera on his hip, waiting. She was at the door now and he watched her open it and start to back through.

"Don't try to follow me. Please. I don't want to have to—"

She did not finish, but slipped into the hall. Casey leaped forward. When he opened the door again she was nearly to the stairs and spun about as she heard him, the tiny automatic coming up and desperation in her eyes.

"It's okay," Casey said and then, not holding up the camera but wedging it on his hip as he had so often done before, he pressed the shutter release.

The sudden explosion of light blinded her. Before she could move, Casey had stepped back into the entry-way and slammed the door. For just another second or so he waited, listening to see if she would come back; when he heard her on the stairs he strode toward the windows at the front of the room and opened one.

"Hey, Augie," he called, sticking out his head. The taxi driver looked up. "Your fare a dame? Okay. There's a fin in it for you if you can find out where she lives."

He closed the window quickly and stood back, peering from the edge of the curtain as the; girl came out and ran to the cab. Seeing it roll away and thinking of his picture he said softly, "Let's see what kind of jam this one gets me into," and would have grinned had he not remembered where he was and what lay behind him on the floor.

The bitterness was hard and implacable in Casey's thoughts as he moved back to the center of the room. Somehow the girl did not worry him as much as he had expected. A guy like Perry Austin would know plenty of girls and if this was one of them she looked like a winner. Later, when he heard from Augie, he'd know where she went and after he'd developed the picture he might find someone who could identify her. Then, if the setup looked sour, he could find out the rest of it. Until then the only thing to do was call Logan and let him get started.

He went over to the desk, wondering if he should call the office and deciding against it when he realized that this would be an afternoon story. He reached for the telephone and then stopped as his eye fell on the center drawer. It was open a couple of inches and he pulled it wide. He could tell from the confusion of papers inside that someone had searched it. The girl? Or someone before her? He was still thinking about it when someone knocked on the door.

Now what? he thought. He took the film holder from the camera and put it in his pocket; then went over and opened the door. Harry Nye was standing there. He looked surprised and sounded that way.

"Oh—hello," he said.

"Hello." Casey just looked at him for a moment, a jumble of new thoughts tangling inside his head as he remembered how Nye had walked in during the police investigation the night before.

"Perry in?"

"Yeah," Casey said, and opened the door. "Come on in." He stood out of the way. Nye passed in front of him and Casey closed the door quietly, watching the man gain the doorway of the living-room and then stop with a jerk that stiffened his neck and shoulders. He did not move until Casey came up beside him. Even then he did not speak, but fixed him with a narrowed stony stare and then moved silently up to the body.

"Twice, huh?" he said finally, as though talking to himself. "And quite a while ago." He walked round the body after he had felt the wrist. He looked at Casey, inspected the room as he reached for a cigarette. Finally he went over to the desk and glanced at the drawer Casey had opened.

All this time Casey said nothing. He watched Nye, thinking, sizing him up, smelling the faint odor of barber's lotion the man had brought into the room. He wore a light camel's-hair coat and an expensive-looking herringbone suit of light gray. His wing-tipped oxfords were nicely polished. He pushed back his hat slightly and brushed his pointed mustache with the knuckle of his forefinger, turning those amber-colored eyes on Casey as he spoke.

"How long you been here?"

"About half an hour."

"How'd you get in?"

"The door was open." Casey moved over to the plate case and took out a fresh film holder. "You get around, don't you?"

"I was thinking the same thing about you." Nye gestured toward the drawer. "Who searched the desk?"

"Who would you think?" Casey watched speculatively, aware of a growing distaste for this man.

"The guy that killed him. Unless it was you."

"It wasn't me."

"Called the cops yet?"

"I was just going to," Casey said. There were more questions he wanted to ask, but he knew Logan could ask them more efficiently. He picked up the telephone and asked for police headquarters.

CHAPTER ELEVEN

A MAN WITH A PAST

THE ROUTINE BUSINESS that immediately follows the discovery of a murder was going on in the living-room, and Lieutenant Logan had left the details in the hands of the headquarters experts while he took Casey and Harry Nye to the kitchen so they would not be bothered. He had accepted Casey's statement as to why he was looking for Perry Austin, but he was not at all satisfied with what Nye had to say.

"You just happened to stop in, huh?"

"That's right, Lieutenant."

"Last night you said Endicott *told* you to stop and see him. This morning it was just coincidence?"

Nye nodded. He was sitting in a chair he had tipped back against the wall, examining his fingernails.

"When'd you see him last?" Logan went on.

"A couple of nights ago, I guess it was," Nye said. "At the Club Berkely."

"A good friend of yours, was he?"

"Well, yes." Nye caressed his mustache. "He knew a lot of good numbers."

"So do you."

Nye grinned. "We'd sometimes go out on dates together."

Logan opened a kitchen cabinet and took out a glass. While he drew a drink of water Casey, sitting there on the kitchen table, decided Logan was getting exactly nowhere with Harry Nye. As for himself Casey had a lot of things he intended to give out, but not in front of the private detective. Somehow the conviction had taken root that Nye had come to Stanford Endicott's office the night before to find out just what progress the police were making and he wondered if the same thing could be true now. Such a supposition presupposed that Nye had either committed the murders, or knew who had. Still—

"We checked on you from eight-thirty till nine last night," Logan was saying.

"Does the alibi stand up?" Nye asked mildly.

"For now it does. Where were you when Austin got his?"

Nye grinned. "I don't know. When did he get it?"

Logan never batted an eye. He must have expected some such answer but Casey gave him credit for trying and for passing right on to the next question.

"You want to give me a statement now or at headquarters?"

"About what?"

"Where you were after nine—until you went to bed."

"It's okay with me any way you want it."

Logan went to the door and yelled down the hall. A sandy-haired fellow with glasses appeared, pulling a stenographer's notebook from his pocket.

"Nye's going to make a statement, Mert," Logan said. "Take it down—if you can find a place to sit. In the bedroom, maybe." He nodded to Nye. "When you finish you can shove off. And if you should happen to remember why you happened to drop in here this morning, let me know."

Nye said okay and trailed out after the stenographer. Casey got up and shut the door.

"He's lying."

"What makes you think so?"

'There's a lot more to this than you know. I can't give any reasons. It's only a hunch but—" He broke off, cocked one brow at Logan. "How do you feel?"

Logan scowled. "What's that got to do with it?"

"I'm going to fix you up good," Casey said, and went on to tell about the picture he had taken the night before and how he had given it to Austin.

A flush crept up Logan's neck and a look of exasperation came over his face. "You held out on me, huh?"

"I didn't know if it would turn out."

"Sure. Somebody swipes your plate case from our car so you sound off to me. Oh, no. You didn't know any reason why anybody should take it. You couldn't think why those two hoods should try to knock you off last night. You were going to play cagey and crack this all yourself. You were going to outsmart the whole damn Department."

Casey let him go until he ran out of breath. He was in the wrong and he knew it, and for once he was willing to accept Logan's wrath without argument.

"I told you how it was," he said. "I got a quick shot of the guy in the sedan. I didn't think it would be much. There wasn't any point in telling you about it until I found out what I had. I told you I'd seen him, didn't I?"

"And didn't know who he was," Logan said.

"I still don't know."

"And when do I start believing you?"

The lash of Logan's anger began to stir Casey's own resentment. "When you get damn good and ready," he said. "I couldn't have turned the picture over to you anyway, could I? I didn't have it, did I?"

"You could have told me Austin had it. We could have started looking for him."

The answer sobered Casey. There it was again. Maybe Austin would be alive if he could have been found in time. If Casey hadn't given him the film holder in the first place— He tried to shake off that overwhelming feeling of guilt, to tell himself that no matter what had happened there was only one thing to be done now: find who killed Austin.

"I'm not going to argue with you," he said. "I didn't give you the picture—"

"Then what're you telling me about it now for?"

"To show you why he was killed."

"Oh." Logan nodded, his tone edged. "Is that it? Well you know how it looks to us, don't you? Austin was up in Endicott's offices alone—when you were out chasing the killer. He'd snoop around, wouldn't he? And suppose he found something that looked good to him. Suppose he went out later with the idea of picking up a little dough on the side?"

Casey looked at him. His broad face was red now and his dark eyes were cold and disgusted. "I understand Navin's building a new house," he said quietly.

Logan took a step forward and stopped, jaw tightening. Casey could have hurt him no more had he slugged him. Navin was attached to the vice squad. Navin was only a detective, but had a better car than Logan's, and a better house. The inference was there and people who got around knew that such things happened. So did Logan. That's why he was bitter about it, knowing that most men in the Department were as honest as himself. "That big mouth'll get you in trouble some day," he lipped.

"Sure," Casey said. "It don't sound so good, does it? Okay. Then lay off Austin. He was no blackmailer. He was no pal of mine but he worked with me. He was a good camera."

Logan went over to the kitchen window and looked out. When he turned much of his wrath had evaporated. "Let's start over," he said. "You don't have to throw that Navin business in my face. I don't say Austin was a blackmailer, I'm only saying it was the only motive I had—until you finally come up with this picture story."

Casey leaned back and felt better. "I didn't hold out because I was trying to outsmart you," he said. "If it had come out, you'd have had it."

Logan nodded. "That must be it," he said. "Somebody found out that Austin had that film holder."

"How did those two hoods get in on it? The killer couldn't have known all this was going to happen. They must have already been in town."

"And the killer knew where to get in touch with them," Logan said. "This thing is beginning to look like something."

Casey told about the call from Nat Garrison.

"That guy is punchy," Logan said.

"It won't stop him from taking pot shots at me. When're you going to pick him up?"

"We'll get him. We need him. If he's tellin' the truth, if he left Endicott alive—and I don't say he did, mind you—he may know plenty because that must mean the killer was already up there in that office."

A knock came on the door then and Sergeant Manahan entered. He had handkerchiefs spread on each palm. In one was the .32 Colt. "This ain't the gun that killed Endicott," he said.

Logan nodded. "The other was a .38."

"And Austin had a permit for a .32 Colt. I don't want to gum things up looking for the number on this until Len gets through, but this might be Austin's."

He put the gun down and spread the other handkerchief. It had two empty shells in it and the rouge-tipped cigarette Casey had seen. Both shells had been bent. Casey recognized the one he had stepped on; the other was practically flat.

Logan grunted disdainfully. "Look at 'em," he said. "A fine crew I've got. The only way they find clues is to step on 'em."

Manahan grinned. "I don't know. We didn't do 'em both. I found one on the desk."

Casey saw no point in saying he had stepped on it and put it there. He kept still, waiting for the reference to the cigarette butt. It came immediately.

"There was a dame around," Manahan said.

Logan picked up the butt. "She could've been here any time."

"Len says there's a woman's prints on the desk. Looked like somebody's been searching it."

Casey sighed but did not realize it until Logan looked at him. "What's your trouble?"

"I'm tired," Casey said, and when Logan continued to Manahan, he realized he was again in the same spot he had been with Lyda Hoyt the night before.

Ever since Logan had arrived he had been thinking about the girl whose picture he took. One reason he turned in more exclusive pictures than any other camera in town was because the police knew he played ball and trusted him because of this. They didn't have to worry about him. They knew he was out to get pictures and not to solve cases. When he had information he passed it along for what it was worth.

This co-operation paid dividends, and yet there were draw-backs; times when he would rather not have had any information whatsoever. It was like this now. He wanted to help Logan and yet he was deliberately withholding vital information. He had done this with Lyda Hoyt's picture last night, and now he found himself doing the same thing again. The reason was clear, but he didn't like to be in the middle this way. Experience had shown him that innocent people became involved in murders and that once involved it was not always easy to extricate themselves without a lot of unpleasant publicity.

Logan was a cop. It was his job to pry into every bit of information that came his way. If he knew about Lyda Hoyt he'd have to question her; perhaps the D.A. would. It was the same with this girl. She knew something and Casey wanted to find out what it was. To tell Logan, to show the picture, would mean that the police would run her down. Some of the newspapers might get it. If she was a material witness, that was one thing, and she'd have to take the publicity that followed. But if she wasn't, if she was just some friend of Austin's—

Casey made up his mind. Right or wrong he knew what he was going to do. Something about that girl impressed him. He liked her looks, the way she held herself. She wasn't any tramp. He'd find out about her first. Then, if he had to, he'd go to Logan. Logan would steam all over again, but in the end it would be all right so long as the information helped the case.

"Okay, Flash." Logan was rising and moving toward the door. "We'll pick up Garrison but—well, watch yourself until we do."

When Casey got back to the *Express*, he found Wade and O'Hearn talking about Austin and he sat down and gave them a brief account of what had happened.

Casey ducked most of the questions they asked, pleading igno-
rance and telling them nothing about his own theory as to the motive
behind the murder. He wanted to develop the picture of the girl he
had surprised in Austin's apartment, but he did not want an audience and he was glad when an assignment came for O'Hearn. To get
rid of Wade, he gave him the second film holder he had exposed in
the apartment, keeping the one with the picture of the girl.

Wade disappeared in the darkroom corridor and Casey went over
to Austin's desk. He sat down, his brow creased and his stare remote.
Finally he tried the desk drawers and found them locked; then something—stubbornness, an unwillingness to give up his search while
any hope remained—drove him out of the studio and down the hall
to the engraving-room where he borrowed a screwdriver.

For a moment as he sat down at Austin's desk again, he hesitated. He told himself this was a crazy idea, but he couldn't convince
himself. There was still a chance that Austin had returned to the
studio last night and left the film holder Casey had entrusted to him
in the desk. He wedged the screwdriver in between the lock and the
frame of the desk and began to pry at the drawer. Seconds later he
had it open.

He glanced through it, looking for a film holder but finding only
papers and bills and a few prints that were of no importance. He
tried another drawer, released now by the forcing of the lock. He
found some notebooks and stationery. In the deep drawer on the
right, he found a steel box and took it out. It was perhaps a foot
long, six inches wide, and three inches deep, and fashioned of heavy,
enameled steel. Putting it aside until he had searched the remaining drawers, he came back to it, turning it over in his hand and
thinking hard.

This was the sort of thing a person would keep his private
papers in—insurance policies, bonds, stock certificates—if he had

any. *He'd never put that film holder in there*, Casey thought. *Why should he?*

At that he experimented with the screwdriver for a few seconds, not trying very hard, feeling pretty guilty about what he was doing. It was with some relief that he decided the steel was too tough to be forced by a screwdriver, and he had put the box back in the lower drawer when the telephone jangled on his desk. He crossed to it, answered it.

"Yes. This is Casey. . . . What? Yes . . . yes, sure. That's great. I'll be right over."

He slammed the telephone down, said, "Hah!" softly, and the worry unfolded temporarily from his brow. He looked round for his coat, grabbed it, and clamped on his hat, then he strode down the darkroom corridor, thrust his head around the corner, and yelled through the blackness of the developing cubicles. "Tom. Just got a call from the hospital. Finell's come around. He wants to see me."

"Hey, wait!" Wade called.

"Wait, hell!" Casey said. "Put those prints on my desk. I'll probably be back in a half-hour."

CHAPTER TWELVE

PICTURES, GOOD AND BAD

FINELL WAS PROPPED UP on a pillow, his face strangely pale under the carroty mop of his hair that jutted out from the two-inch bandage on his head. His grin was quick and broad when Casey stamped into the room and stopped beside the bed.

"Hyuh, boy."

"Hy, Flash."

"How's the head?"

"Okay. I think I could get up if they'd let me."

"You're crazy." Casey pulled up a chair and sat down, fanning out his coat. "Can you smoke?"

Finell said he could and Casey lit a cigarette for him.

"What happened? Who slugged you?"

"I don't know, Flash." Finell's grin fled. "I was just coming in—"

"Didn't you see the guy?"

"Yes, but—"

"Okay," Casey said. "You tell it."

"It was about twelve-fifteen, I think. Blaine sent me out on a fire and a fireman got hurt and I stuck around, that's why I was so late. I came in and saw somebody bending over your desk."

"Oh."

Finell glanced at him, hesitated, then went on. "For just a second I thought it was you and then I knew it wasn't because he wasn't big enough. I may have said something. I'm not sure." Finell spread his hands. "That's all. The guy turned and then, wham! Out went the lights."

"In your head?"

"Yeah. There must have been another one. I didn't see him."

"The guy at the desk didn't hit you?"

"No. I was looking at him when it happened."

Casey got up, walked over to the door, came back and sat down. "We found you in the printing-room about fifteen or twenty minutes later, I guess. They must have dragged you in there out of the way. What did the guy look like? The one at the desk?"

Finell glanced out the window. "I only got a glimpse of him when the ceiling fell on me but I think he was thin, about medium height. I think he had a dark hat on." Finell looked distressed. "I can't seem to remember anything else."

"Did he have a funny-looking nose?"

Finell snapped his fingers. "Yes. Yes, sure he did."

"Like what?"

"Kinda flat at the bottom and"—he paused and put his finger to the bridge of his nose—"up here it looked like a piece had been hammered out of it."

"You'll do," Casey said. "You got the eye, boy." And then the soberness was on him again and he said, "I think we got him—and his pal, too."

Finell wanted details but Casey didn't want to tire him unnecessarily and merely said the police had picked them up. He didn't know what they were doing in the studio. A couple of prowlers probably, he said, but all the time things were adding up in his mind and he knew that the gunmen tied in with the rest of his theory. They had stolen his plate case, brought it back when the picture they wanted was missing. Finell had walked in on them while they were forcing open his desk. They'd found the picture of Lyda and taken it.

"Did you see Perry Austin last night?" he asked.

"Yes."

Casey sat up. "When?"

"Oh—about nine-thirty. He was there about a half-hour or so."

Casey digested this. He took a breath. He asked the next question quietly, as though he was afraid of it. "Did he say anything about a film holder of mine?"

Finell grinned. "Sure."

Casey waited, holding his breath.

"He gave it to me," Finell said.

"What?"

Finell looked startled. "He told me I was to hang on to it. He told me I shouldn't leave it around."

Casey swallowed. He tried to keep his voice steady and not get Finell all upset. "What'd you do with it?"

"Put it in my pocket."

"What pocket?"

"Of my topcoat. That one." He nodded toward the gray raglan hanging on the rack in the corner. "He told me not to leave it—the film holder, I mean—so when I went out—"

Casey got up, overturning the chair. He went over to the topcoat and slid his hands along the pockets; then something snapped inside his chest and all the tension went out along with his breath and he had the film holder, looking at it curiously for a moment as though he still did not believe it. He came back and sat down, grinning a little now with relief, wondering how he was going to explain things to Finell.

Finell was watching him closely. He looked worried. "What's wrong, Flash? Did I pull a boner?"

"Anything else you could have done with it would have been a boner," Casey said. "What you did was perfect." He felt the cigarette burn his fingers and put it in an ash tray. He was still a little incredulous as he looked down at the film holder; he tucked it in his pocket.

"Look," he said, "I got a lot of gabbing to do. You all right? If you don't feel so hot I'll come back."

"No." Finell's gaze was bright with interest. "I'm swell, Flash. Go ahead."

So Casey told him, taking his time, keeping his voice level, going back to the murder of Stanford Endicott and explaining what had happened. In the end he also told him what was on the film holder.

"It's under your hat," he said. "And maybe I shouldn't tell you at all. But you got slugged because of that picture and I guess you have a right to know."

Finell listened, his gaze intent, his lips parted until Casey started to tell him about Perry Austin and what had happened that morning; then, gradually, the paleness crept back into his face and his jaw began to sag. "Oh," he said finally. "Jeeze, poor Perry. When those two hoods couldn't find the film they went after him, knowing, somehow, that he'd been up to Endicott's with you. They're the ones, aren't they? Those two?"

Casey said he didn't know. "We won't know, either, until an autopsy shows when Austin died. If it wasn't them it was the guy that hired them." He leaned back, watching Finell, giving him a chance to get used to the idea and steady down.

"Tell me about last night," he said presently. "Just what happened from the time Perry came in until you got slugged?"

"Well, like I said, he came in and gave me the film holder and told me to be sure I gave it to you. Then he said he had some copying to do and not to bother him."

"Copying?" Casey frowned, knowing what Finell meant and thinking about the apparatus on the table at one end of the corridor next to the printing-room. It was simply a camera and an easel so set up that any print or document could be readily photographed and reproduced again on another negative. The camera could be moved back and forth horizontally and the subject to be copied was pinned to the easel or stuck there with rubber cement. Casey scratched his head. "What was he copying? You know?"

Finell said he didn't.

"Did he develop the negatives he took?"

"I think so. He developed something, anyway."

"He didn't print anything? Then what did he do with the negatives?"

"I don't know, Flash." Finell grinned sheepishly. "I wasn't paying any attention. I was reading the *Racing Form*. Along about ten I went out to the can and kidded around with Murphy and when I got back to the studio, Austin was just coming out."

Casey swallowed his disappointment and said, "Okay. Then what?"

"I sat around till I got the call from Blaine to cover the fire."

"And you took the holder with you," Casey said, realizing that Finell must have left shortly before he arrived.

"Well, sure. It was early. I didn't expect to be gone more'n an hour, and Austin said not to leave it around, and then that fireman got hurt. I phoned in and Blaine said to stick with it. That's why I didn't get back until late."

Casey got up, shaking his head. "That's the breaks for you," he grumbled. "If you'd left twenty minutes later I'd've seen you. If the fireman hadn't got hurt I'd've seen you." He pushed the chair out of the way, snorting disgustedly. "And all the time you had the lousy holder in your pocket. Hell, I even took the coat off you and used it for a pillow. I told Wade to bring it out here so you'd have it. Well—" He put a grin on and looked down at Finell. "You did all right," he said.

Casey took his time with the four pieces of cut film he unloaded from the two holders in the darkroom cubicle. Two of those pieces of film didn't matter—one was of Endicott and one was of Austin—but the other two—

He made fresh developer and got a new fixing bath to be sure he could get the most out of the film. He wasn't worried about the one he had taken of the girl outside Austin's apartment, but the other, the one he'd taken the night before of the fleeing sedan, would need all the forcing he could give it.

He was pretty nervous, waiting for the film to fix. He could tell then that the quality of the negative was all right, but he could not be sure of details until he printed it. He chain-smoked while he waited for the film to dry and then put it in the enlarger and slid a piece of paper in the easel. He watched the image spring to life in the developer, timing it, shoving it into the water and then into the hypo, not daring really to examine it until it had been there a minute or so. When, finally, he held it up under the orange light he knew what he had: just what he had expected.

He dropped the print back in the hypo, cursing softly, feeling his hope and anticipation slip away and the weariness close down on him. It was a good print, all right. A bit thin because he'd only used one flash bulb and he'd been quite a distance from the sedan, but strong enough to show the car clearly, the edge of a man's hat, a thin slice of the face that was half-turned toward him.

"I could blow it up the size of the room," he said bitterly, "and still I wouldn't have enough to know who he was." He picked up the print again. "And look at the angle," he added, inspecting the quartering shot. "Can't even see the license tag."

After that Casey had a bad few minutes. It was tough to stand there and make prints when all the time you were thinking that Austin had been killed for nothing, that the picture that had cost him his life hadn't been worth a damn and that if you had hung onto it yourself, he would still be alive.

He made two more prints automatically—the one of Endicott that had been on the holder with the shot of the sedan, and the one he had taken of Austin lying there on the floor. When he came to the negative of the girl with the gun he had to think of other things and that helped.

This was a picture he expected to show here and there for purposes of identification, and he knew he couldn't offer it as it was because of the gun in her hand. So he masked off the lower part of her body, adjusted the enlarger, and made an eight-by-ten print of her head and shoulders. It came out nicely. Anyone that knew her would recognize her from this likeness.

Elsie Andrews, the society editor of the *Express*, was a smart-looking woman, no longer young, but with good features and a pleasant manner. She wasn't pretty, but she had a nice smile and gave it to Casey when he perched on the corner of her desk and handed her the picture of the girl.

"Ever see her before?"

Elsie Andrews inspected the photograph, reaching absently for a pack of cigarettes on her desk. Presently she looked up. "Yes, I have."

"Know her?"

"I should." She caught one lip between her teeth and stared. "At least I think I should. Wait a minute."

She rose and left the office. When she came back she was smiling. "I thought I did," she said. "Nancy Jamison."

"Society?"

"Rather. She's General Jamison's daughter." She looked at the picture again. "What'd you do to her? She looks pretty frightened about something."

"Oh, that." Casey swallowed and grinned. "I guess I startled her." He reached out for the picture. "Thanks, Elsie— Oh, what's she do, anyway? Just another deb or—"

"She paints. And rather well too, I understand. She's had a couple of one-man shows."

Casually, Casey pursued his questioning, and among other things he learned that Nancy Jamison had an apartment of her own somewhere on the Hill, that she had a brother only recently graduated from West Point, and that while she had the proper requisites, she did not seem to care greatly for the obligations that a strictly social life entailed. She was seldom in the news, seldom seen at first nights or charity affairs, seldom photographed.

"Just what," Elsie Andrews asked, pushing her elbows on the desk as she finished and giving Casey that nice smile, "are you trying to promote?"

Casey colored. "Nothing," he said. "She—she's sort of nice, that's all. I just wondered who she was." And then he thanked her and backed out of her office, taking the photograph with him.

The telephone was ringing when he reached the studio. It was MacGrath, the managing editor. "Come on up," he said. "I want to talk to you."

Casey picked up the two prints of Austin Wade had made for him, the one of the fleeing sedan, the one he himself had brought from Austin's apartment, the one of Endicott taken the night before. He put the one of the sedan with the one of the girl. He rolled them up, put them far back in the bottom drawer, and piled some books in front of them. The others he took with him, climbing the stairs and crossing the city room, practically empty at this hour, to a private office in one corner.

MacGrath was busy signing some letters when Casey entered, and did not look up but said, "Sit down, Flash," and kept on writing.

Casey took the worn leather chair by the window. He looked out and watched a transport plane glide swiftly across the cloudless sky; then he looked back at MacGrath, watching him read the letters and swivel the half-smoked cigar that seemed to form an integral part of his features. Presently the letters were finished and put aside. MacGrath leaned back in his chair—or started to—and then he caught sight of the prints in Casey's hand.

"What are those?" he asked and looked at them quickly, interest kindling in his deep-set eyes. He glanced at Casey, looked at the prints again, pointing to the one of Endicott. "You're a little late with that one, aren't you? If we'd had that last night—"

"It would have been good, huh?" Casey said.

MacGrath took the cigar from his mouth, examined it, replaced it in the opposite corner. He was a blunt-jawed man, thick-necked, stocky. Like Blaine he was a driver, but his methods were different and where the city editor was sarcastic and ironic in manner, MacGrath was direct, impatient, but always fair because he had a vast understanding of men.

"Every time I get ready to ride you," he said, "you show up with some pictures and make a chump out of me. Where've you been? What've you been doing? You were out all night on this Endicott thing and getting pushed around by a couple of thugs and not a picture do we get out of you."

He reached for a copy of the final edition. On the front page was a picture taken the night before of the two gunmen standing in the headlights of their car. The caption said they were being held in connection with the murder of Stanford Endicott. "Wade took this," MacGrath said. "Where were you?"

"Sitting on the bumper with a gun in my hand."

"Wade said you wouldn't let him get you in the shot. Camera shy?"

Casey grinned and made noises in his throat. MacGrath sat up, a seriousness cloaking his blunt face. "What about Perry Austin?"

Casey told what he knew. He told about the picture of the fleeing sedan. He explained how Finell had taken it away and he said he believed Perry Austin had been killed because of it.

"Where is it?"

Casey hesitated, deciding not to show it because he was afraid MacGrath might print it anyway. Until he actually saw it, the killer could not know what was on the film and that uncertainty was something Casey wanted to maintain.

"It didn't come out," he said.

"What?" MacGrath scowled at him. "Since when are you taking pictures that don't come out?"

"I was too far away. I got the car, but no number and it would never reproduce on newsprint anyway."

MacGrath opened his mouth and Casey got ready for further argument when the telephone rang. "Yeah? Yes. He's here now. . . . For you," he said, and handed the instrument to Casey.

"Casey?" The voice was Lieutenant Logan's and it came across the wire curt and hard. "I want to see you."

"Okay," Casey said. "As soon as I finish—"

"Finish, hell," Logan snapped. "I want to see you now. Do you want to come or shall I send for you?"

Casey choked back an angry retort. What was the use of scrapping over a telephone? "I'll be over," he said and hung up, glowering for a moment until he became aware of MacGrath's stare. "Logan," he said. "He wants to see me. He sounded a little sore."

MacGrath let him get to the door before he said, "About this Austin business. We're going to offer a reward. He was one of our boys. We ought to do what we can." He paused, chewing on the cigar. "He wasn't my kind of man, but Blaine said he was a good camera."

"He was," Casey said.

MacGrath waved him out. "If you find out anything that might help, let me in on it. When they start knocking off my cameras it's time I did a little crowding on my own. Stick with it, Flash. Whatever you do, I'm backing you, understand?"

Casey said he did and went out, grateful that he had a man like MacGrath for a boss.

CHAPTER THIRTEEN
SMOOTH SUSPECT

LIEUTENANT LOGAN HAD A MODEST OFFICE with a roll-top desk, three chairs—not including the desk chair—a table, and a hat rack, all in golden oak that had mellowed by usage and age into ordinary, nondescript wood. He was at the window staring out when Casey entered without knocking, and the instant the photographer saw the lean, tight face he knew he was in for a session.

"I was just going to send for you," Logan said.

"Then I saved the city some dough," Casey said, his tone as blunt as Logan's. "What do you want?"

Logan stepped past the desk to a door connecting with an adjoining room, and threw it open. "Come in, please."

He stepped back and then Casey saw her, felt the cool sweep of her blue eyes as she hesitated on the threshold. After that he was too confused to grasp the full significance of Lyda Hoyt's presence here, and what happened after that was a complication of many things he did not understand until later.

He saw Grant Forrester behind her, even as he heard Logan say, "If you'll sit here, Miss Hoyt." He saw Forrester reach out and take his arm. They were close to the doorway then and he heard the fellow say, "In here, if you don't mind." Then he was suddenly being pulled into the next room and the door slammed behind him and Forrester was turning the key.

Not until then did Casey get a legitimate reaction. Surprise was still uppermost in his brain but he saw angry lights in Forrester's eyes, the thin, hard mouth, heard him say, "All right, Casey. This is where you take a licking. Put up your hands."

"Wait a minute." Casey's thick face warped in bewilderment. Before he could speak again the straight left caught him, jarring his cheekbone and knocking him off balance. "Listen," he said.

The left jabbed again in his face, pushing him still farther off balance. He flung out his hand to steady himself, felt his wrist watch smash against the radiator; then he saw Forrester advancing, guard up, and knew he'd better quit talking.

He slipped the next jab, caught the following right on his elbow, and swiveled away. He circled, thinking about this crazy man and his record as a boxer, of his social position and background. Suddenly Casey was furious and as Forrester jabbed the left again, the fury became a cold and collected force that goaded him to action.

He could hear Logan pounding on the door and shouting. He slid his left foot forward. Forrester hit him twice without a return and Casey knew what he was up against. He moved in, watching the left, knowing Forrester was trying to set him up for a solid right-hand smash. When it flicked out again Casey did not try to block, but took it clean and crossed his right, the only way he knew to beat that kind of a punch.

It was a little high, that right; he knew that as it hit and he felt the welcome jolt in his forearm. But it was solid and Casey's weight was behind it, and Forrester went down, stiffly, his feet practically anchored and falling in one piece. He wasn't out. He rolled over and came to one knee. Casey waited, aware of a new noise and commotion behind him. Before Forrester could rise, Logan was between them, and somebody was helping Forrester, and two plain-clothes men were holding Casey's arms.

Logan was apoplectic and for a moment could not find his voice. He glared at Casey, glared harder at Forrester, snapped an order to the plain-clothes men, who then let go of Casey. No one said anything more until the others had left the room.

"I'm sorry, Lieutenant." Forrester brushed himself off. "I couldn't help it."

"We don't go for that sort of thing," Logan said coldly. "It would have served you right if we'd let him cool you off."

"I'm willing to let him try again," Forrester said.

"Yah!" Logan jeered. "He'd knock you silly."

"I still will," Casey said.

Logan spun. "Not here, you won't," he said, jabbing his finger against Casey's chest.

"We can find a place," Forrester said, and somehow Casey liked him for that, in spite of what had happened.

"For now," said Logan, "you'll go in the other room and sit down." He went over to the connecting door and unlocked it. "Start something again and I'll have you both thrown in the tank. And if you don't think I can, Mr. Forrester—at least until you get a lawyer to spring you—"

"I'm sure you can," Forrester said, and went into the other room and sat down beside Lyda Hoyt, who waited, white and composed.

"I'm sorry, Lyda," he said, quietly. "I—I lost my temper when I saw him."

"I know, darling," she said, and slipped her hand in his.

Logan shut the door and sat down at his desk. His color was still high, his mouth taut. He picked something from his desk and handed it to Casey without looking at it.

"Ever see that before?"

Casey took it. It was a photograph. which had been folded down the middle. He thought he knew what it was, but he didn't want to believe it, he didn't want to look at it; instead he glanced at Forrester and Lyda Hoyt.

"Well," Logan snapped. "Look at it."

Casey did. And seeing that picture of Lyda Hoyt he had locked in his desk the night before, a curious sense of resignation came over him to mix with his bewilderment. He didn't try to figure it out, but handed it back to Logan. "Where'd you get it?"

"In the mail." Logan held up an envelope, across which had been printed in crude penciled letters his name. "This morning." He put the picture and envelope on the desk. He leaned back, watching Casey narrowly. "So you held out again?"

"Yeah," Casey said. "I held out. What about it?"

"What about it?" Logan looked indignant.

"Sure," Casey said. "Let's get straight. I work for the *Express*. They pay me pretty well for taking pictures. But even on them I hold out sometimes. I take pictures that I find out may do more harm than good. That one there is one I held out—until I found out some things. And if I can hold out on MacGrath and the *Express* I can hold out on you."

Logan sputtered a moment. "That ain't the point," he said. "She was at Endicott's last night." He pointed at Lyda Hoyt. "You knew it and you didn't tell me."

"All right," said Casey. "I didn't tell you."

Logan had more to say on the subject and Casey let him go. He knew how it was with Logan. Logan was a cop and a good one. He had a job to do and he did it to the best of his ability, playing no favorites. He wasn't sore about the picture, as such; what annoyed him was that he found himself suddenly confronted with a new angle to a murder case that he might never have known about, had it not been for this picture which had come through the mail.

"Look," Casey said finally. "If I'd told you Miss Hoyt was there last night, what would you have done?"

"Done? Why, I'd have gone to see her—asked her—"

"Well, go ahead. You got her now. Ask her."

"It's not your fault I got her," Logan said. "And I intend to ask her. But first I'm asking you. Where's the negative of that picture?"

Casey thought it over. There it was again. That's what happened when you did favors for people. He remembered the things Jim Bishop had told him the night before and looked at Lyda Hoyt. She was sitting very straight in her chair, her hands in her lap. She wore a simple cloth coat and a little hat about the size of a saucer. She did not seem pretty now, nor even beautiful, and he knew why. What made her beautiful was her personality, the vitality that projected itself across the footlights so that every man and most women in the audience got the idea she was putting on the show for his benefit. He could remember only two comediennes who could do that trick— Gertrude Lawrence and Ethel Merman.

But she wasn't on the stage now. There wasn't any musical background, nor any scenery save this drab office. She couldn't sing a song now, or laugh, or speak bright lines. She had to sit there and wait for him to speak, and try to signal him with her eyes because she was afraid. He knew that and he knew why. Jim Bishop must have told her about his trip to see Casey; now she knew that Casey could tell the truth and smash a secret she and Jim Bishop had decided to keep—the secret of their relationship. She knew what had happened to the negative, but she could not tell Forrester or Logan; she could do nothing now but sit there and watch him.

It would have saved her much anguish had she really known Casey. She would have had no cause to worry then. Having made a commitment to Jim Bishop, nothing could make the big photographer renege except the certain knowledge that she had actually done the murder. He smiled at her with his eyes and said to Logan, "I destroyed it."

Logan closed one eye. "Yes, you did."

"Okay." Casey leaned back and lit a cigarette.

"What for?" Logan said when he realized no elaboration was coming.

"It was dynamite. I didn't want to leave it around."

"You kept the print."

"Yeah. Because I wasn't sure what the score was then. I locked it in my desk. And those two new boarders of yours cracked the lock and grabbed it. Ask them about it."

"I will."

"Is that the truth?" Grant Forrester leaned forward. He had a mouse under one eye and a blue lump on his cheekbone, all from that one punch, and seeing this, Casey felt compensated for the soreness in his own face.

"You thought I mailed it in?" he said.

Forrester flushed. "I—that is—I didn't know what else to think."

Casey shook his head. "That ought to make me quite a guy."

Forrester's flush was crimson now and he went ahead quickly. "Miss Hoyt called and said she'd been asked to come down here. I came along and when we walked in the lieutenant produced the picture and—I knew you took it and—" He broke off as Logan cut in.

"All right. Never mind that now." He looked at Lyda Hoyt. "I guess the picture doesn't matter much. Whoever sent it had an idea it would make a nice fat red herring. It would have been a lot simpler if I'd known about it but—the important thing, Miss Hoyt, is this: what was your business with Stanford Endicott?"

"I don't believe she has to answer that here, Lieutenant," Forrester said.

"No, she doesn't." Logan pinned him down with steady eyes. "But we're not quite sure of the motive behind that murder. I'm afraid that a grand jury might want to know why Miss Hoyt had to see Endicott last night. Why she had to hurry there during intermission; why she could not wait to see him until this morning."

"Yes," Lyda Hoyt said. "I see what you mean." She glanced down at her gloved hands. When she looked up again, her eyes met Casey's for an instant and he saw she wasn't afraid any more. There was a softness there, a fleeting impression of gratitude; then the moment was gone and she was looking at Logan. "I can tell you what my business was."

"Lyda!" Forrester said.

"It's all right." She smiled at him. "There's no reason why you shouldn't know," she said, and then Casey realized that she had not told Forrester what this business was either.

"It concerns a very dear friend of mine," she began. "An old friend—who got in trouble with the police many years ago. You know of such people, don't you, Lieutenant? Men and women who have slipped once and come a cropper when young and have never made a misstep since?"

Logan nodded. "We have a whole file full of such cases. A locked file, Miss Hoyt, so that no one can ever use that record against them."

"Yes— Well, it's like that with—my friend. It happened ten years ago. She was out with a boy—I'm not going to give you details—and he tried to hold up a jewelry store. She hadn't known the boy but a few days, had been dancing and to the movies with him, but that made no difference to the authorities. They were both arrested. He went to prison and she was sentenced to the House of Correction for a year, but on the way there was an accident and she ran away."

She paused to wet her lips before she continued. "Somehow, she found a job—she had no family—and later managed to make a place for herself in the theater. That's how I happened to know her. I never knew the story until a few weeks ago and I think she told me because—well, the past was more than ever on her mind. She had married. She has money and position. She is about to have a baby. And although she knew that the chances were that the past would stay dead, there was in her mind the possibility that it would not.

"You see, it wasn't just that she had a record. That would not have been so bad, since she would have paid any debt she owed. But she had not paid. For all she knew there was still this sentence hanging over her. Every now and then she would read in the papers about some man being taken away to serve sentence—or to stand trial—for something that had happened years ago. So she came to me. She wanted a pardon so she could have peace of mind, and she was willing to take the risk of getting one. I went to Mr. Endicott. He got it for her, quietly—this all happened in the Middle West— and came back yesterday."

"I see," Logan said, but, watching him, Casey still saw traces of doubt in the angles of his eyes. "And you went to his office between performances—"

"It sounds silly now, doesn't it?" Lyda Hoyt smiled faintly and unfolded her hands. "I know it does. He phoned me around dinner time but it was too late then. And during the first act—well, I read that he'd been arrested and that worried me and"—she caught her lip—"the impulse struck me and I obeyed it. I didn't I want anything to happen now after all our trouble, and I knew I'd have time—so I went."

"But you didn't get it," Logan said.

"No. And that has worried me even more than the picture that Mr. Casey took. I was afraid you might find something that—" She

SILENT ARE THE DEAD

broke off and took a breath. "You haven't found it, have you? That pardon?"

Logan said he hadn't, and what was her friend's name. When she said she would not tell, he asked how he was to know if the police did find the documents.

"Mr. Endicott told me it would be in an envelope," Lyda Hoyt said. "He said he'd put my name on it and if I should come and he wasn't in, I could get it from his secretary."

There wasn't much left for Logan to say. He asked a few more questions and then nodded and rose. "All right," he said. "I'll let you know if we run across the envelope, Miss Hoyt. And you needn't worry about this picture of Casey's. I'll keep it locked up for a few days and perhaps by then I can return it to you."

He opened the door. "If I were you, Mr. Forrester," he said dryly, "I'd pick somewhere else for my boxing exhibitions. I think I'd stay in my own class too. Casey's a bad guy to have sore at you."

"I hope he won't be," Forrester said. He gave Casey his hand. "I'm sorry, old man. I hope we can be friends. I'm afraid I ruined that watch of yours but I'll replace it if you—"

"That's okay," Casey said. "I bust it all the time."

Lyda Hoyt came up to him and offered her hand. "We're closing the show this week," she said, and hesitated, and he saw that the blue in her eyes was soft and moist. "Could you come and see me before I go, please?"

Casey had to clear his throat. "Sure," he said gruffly. "I'd like to," he said.

Logan grew thoughtful when the door had closed and he returned to his chair. "There's a woman for you," he said. "She's not pretty, but she's got something. Class or something. You can feel it. It sticks out all over her."

"You mean you like her," Casey said.

"Yes, you louse."

Casey unstrapped his watch and looked at the smashed face. He dropped it in his pocket, sighed, touched the bruises on his cheek. "Me too," he said.

Sergeant Manahan came in. "Bernie Dixon's downstairs," he said.

"Bring him up," Logan said.

"Dixon, huh?" Casey looked interested. "Finding out things?"

"Lots of things." Logan sucked his lips and traced a circle in the dust on his desk. "Lots of things. It's beginning to look like Endicott had his finger in other things besides hot bonds."

"And you figure Endicott—"

"We don't know—yet."

"And you haven't picked up Garrison yet either, have you?"

"No, damn it!"

The door opened and Manahan came in with Bernie Dixon. He looked like a million dollars, sartorially speaking.

"Good morning, Lieutenant. Or is it afternoon? Casey, how are you?"

Logan said hello and sit down, and Casey said he was all right. Dixon unbuttoned the smooth-fitting gray coat, took a chair and crossed his legs, reaching for a cigarette case as he did so.

"What's on your mind?" he said. "And what's this about Perry Austin?"

Logan said they weren't sure yet. "We've got a couple of hoods from Jersey downstairs that may know something about it," he said, "but for now—"

"From Jersey?" Dixon blew smoke toward the ceiling. "What're they doing here?"

"That's what we're going to find out," Logan said. "And who hired 'em."

Dixon was very much at ease. He hooked one arm across the

chair back and swung his leg on the other knee. He got very cozy, asking questions, and Casey, watching Logan, could see irritation and resentment creeping into the lieutenant's dark eyes; he knew that Logan's opinion of Dixon was the same as his own: that for all his present polish and success, Dixon was still a racketeer.

"You figure they knocked off Endicott?" Dixon asked.

"Maybe, maybe not. Maybe they were hired *after* Endicott was shot—to cover up, one way or another."

"You mean they were hiding out in town?"

"That's exactly what I mean. We're finding out a lot of things about Endicott we didn't know, but that's not why I asked you to stop in." He leaned back in his chair, studying Dixon with steady eyes. "What I want from you is where were you last night between eight and nine-thirty?"

Dixon smiled, or thought he did. He had practically no lips and be generally kept them closed so that his mouth was just a line that curved in various directions, depending on his mood. Now it curved up at one corner. "You mean you want an alibi? Well, I happen to have one."

"Where were you?"

"With someone."

"Who?"

Dixon shook his head, lips still curved. "That I can't tell you now."

"A woman?"

"Yes."

Logan chewed this awhile. "You can be made to tell."

"Maybe."

"Mrs. Endicott?"

Dixon uncrossed his legs and stood up, nothing changing in his face. "If I have to, I can tell you," he said. "But I don't have to tell you now— Was that all you wanted, Lieutenant? I've got a busy afternoon."

Logan turned back to his desk, a muscle twitching at the hinge of his jaw. "Okay, Bernie," he said. "Beat it."

Logan watched the door close, his lids coming down and the lines of his face set. He sat that way for quite a while before he said, "He could be our boy. He might have been with Mrs. Endicott—they say he's been cuttin' corners there—but he could still be our boy. Endicott had a pretty fancy organization, and Dixon is the kind of a guy that could have pulled a lot of strings."

Casey waited, wondering what Logan meant by organization. When he saw that there wasn't going to be any further explanation he reached for his hat. He was thinking so hard he went out without bothering to say good-by.

CHAPTER FOURTEEN

AN ORDEAL FOR CASEY

AUGIE, THE TAXI DRIVER, pulled to a stop halfway up the hill and waved proudly toward a somewhat dismal-looking red-brick house that was built flush with the sidewalk. "There you are," he said. "Pay me."

Casey got out and gave the house the once-over. It was a three-storied, age-crusted affair, plain, no different from its neighbors except for the color of the trim on the door. He took out a five-dollar bill, squinted one eye at Augie. "How do I know she's here?"

"That's where I brought her."

"I said I'd give you a fin if you found out where she lived." He paused, watching Augie's face cloud. "And anyway, you're not so damn smart. I even found out what her name is."

"Well, hell—" Augie began.

"Here." Casey gave him the bill. "If I'm not out in five minutes that means you're right. Only"—he winked—"you have to take the fare out."

He tried the door, found it unlocked, and stepped into a flagstone-floored vestibule with six name cards on the wall. After a glance, he went up three steps to another door, opened it, and started climbing.

Nancy Jamison lived on the top floor and Casey was wheezing a little as he knocked on one of the two doors at the head of the stairs. When he saw the knob turn he stepped close, not sure what he was going to say, but determined to get in.

She opened the door herself, and he saw the lashes snap back, the quick surprise in her hazel eyes. He saw her red lips form an O and heard her gasp; then he heard a lot of voices and looked into the room beyond.

There were at least 20 people there, mostly women, standing around with plates in their hands and talking their heads off, looking over at him and then letting the conversation trail off into silence. Casey got his hat off before confusion made him mute. He glanced at the girl and saw her shoulders come back and her chin lift. Her mouth tightened and then, suddenly, she was offering her hand and saying, loud enough for all to hear, "Oh, how nice. How very good of you to come."

Casey wanted to run but he couldn't make his legs move. He felt her firm warm hand in his, knew he was being drawn into the room. As she closed the door he had to turn to get out of her way and she leaned toward him, spoke softly. "What's your name?"

"Casey."

"I'll take your things," she said, her voice normal once more.

She reappeared, smiling. "Now come along and meet some people, Mr. Casey," she said. The next few minutes became a lifetime of sheer agony for Casey. He moved as in a trance, the girl's hand on his arm, mumbling names and saying, "How do you do," over and over and feeling the sweat on his face and the burning in his neck and ears.

"You'd like a drink, wouldn't you?" Nancy Jamison said. "Or"—he wondered if there was a smile in her eyes—"would you prefer tea?"

"A drink, please," Casey said.

"Cocktail or highball?"

"Scotch would be fine."

"Scotch, Norine," she told the maid and then, smiling up at Casey, "Now if you'll excuse me—"

He turned to look over the other guests. The four or five men present were sleek and middle-aged, and they had cornered every woman that was young and attractive. A trio of angular females drifted around him before he realized it.

"Do you paint, Mr. Casey?" one of them asked.

Casey said he didn't and for a moment that killed further conversation.

"Or sculpt?" an efficient-looking person with horn-rimmed glasses ventured hopefully.

"I'm a photographer," Casey said.

"Oh." The three exchanged glances and one of them tried again. "Portraits?"

"Newspaper."

That fixed everything up. "How interesting," they said and drifted off.

It was nearly dark when the last guest had gone and Nancy Jamison closed the door. The maid had started to clean up the room, but Nancy told her to forget it for now and get things in order in the kitchen. Casey, standing wearily by the big easel in the corner, watched her go to the table and pour herself a short drink. She came over to him, glass in hand. "Have a good time?"

He looked at her and grinned, studying the clean young line of her mouth, the smooth skin at her throat. She wore a simple black dress with a touch of white at the neckline and cuffs. Her hair, he saw, was parted at the side and falling softly nearly to her shoulders. She looked tired, and he thought about how he had come here and how expertly she had passed him off as a guest. He found himself admiring her spirit and ready self-reliance and knew that no matter what her story was, he was for her.

"Swell time," he said. "Only these kind of things are hard on your feet."

"Yes," she said, and motioned him to a chair while she sank down on the studio couch. She looked at him, her glance appraising. After a few seconds she said, "How did you find me?"

He told her.

"I see," she said. "Well—"

"I wanted to find out what you were doing in Perry Austin's apartment."

"You're not a policeman?"

"No. But Perry worked on the *Express* with me. I think he was killed because he was doing something for me. I want to find out who did it."

"And you think I did?"

"No, I don't. But you were at his place last night. You were there this morning. That sort of indicates you know something about him."

"Does it?"

He made no answer, but waited, knowing she would speak again.

"I wasn't at his place last night," she said. "I went there and knocked. I had already turned away when you came up the stairs."

"How'd you get in this morning?"

She was inspecting her drink. He thought she smiled. "I was very nice to the janitor. I said Mr. Austin had asked me to wait for him. I smiled and fluttered my eyes. He unlocked the door for me."

"Why?" Casey asked. "Why did you want to get in?"

"I wanted to search it."

"For what?"

She finished her drink and put the glass aside. She asked if he had a cigarette and he gave her one. She inhaled and picked a piece of tobacco from her tongue before she said, "Was Mr. Austin a friend of yours? I mean, did you think a great deal of him?"

"No," Casey said. "Why?"

"Because," Nancy Jamison said, and now her voice was clipped and cold, "Mr. Austin was blackmailing my brother."

Casey sat up, his face stiffening, incredulous. For a moment he could only stare and then his brows screwed down and he tried to laugh. It didn't come off because something in the girl's tone killed it, froze it in his throat.

"You're crazy," he said finally.

"No."

"Not Austin," Casey said. "Austin was no blackmailer."

"He blackmailed my brother—or tried to," Nancy Jamison said flatly.

Casey stood up. He walked round the room and sat down again. It couldn't be. Nobody on the *Express* would blackmail anyone. Every news-photographer had plenty of opportunities but—

"I think you're wrong," he said, his voice quiet now, measured, serious. "I wish you'd tell me about it."

"My brother's in the army. He hasn't had his commission long," Nancy Jamison said, and as she went on, Casey realized he had heard the story before. Not exactly this way, not with the same characters, but fundamentally there was nothing new about it.

Her brother, Fred, had been home on leave, had been one of a party of five that had gone night-clubbing. He was an odd man, his own girl having been asked out to dinner with her parents, and he'd been pretty glum about it so he had taken more to drink than he should. Later he had left the party and disappeared, and although he was not quite sure what had happened, he had apparently been picked up by some girl at the bar and had taken her home.

"He remembered that part," Nancy Jamison said, "but he didn't know about anything else until he saw the picture." She hesitated, continued with an effort. "A picture of a girl in negligee sitting on his lap with her arms around his neck. And Fred with his hair tousled and his coat open and— Oh!" She shuddered, clenching her teeth. "You could see he was drunk and didn't know what he was doing."

"A frame, huh?" Casey's voice was sullen. He had known that was coming by the time she was halfway through. But Austin? No. He couldn't swallow it. "What's the rest of it?" he said.

"A few days later a man came around to see Fred and showed him the picture."

"Austin?"

"Yes. That is, I think so."

Casey's face lit up. "Hah! You think so."

"Please," Nancy Jamison said. "Let me finish. This man came to Fred. I never saw him. He said Fred could have the negative and print for a thousand dollars. Fred came to me because it was the last day of his leave. He had no thousand dollars; neither did I, but I told Fred to tell the man I could get it.

"When me man called up, Fred said he had to return to camp, but that I would pay. He left a number for me to call and I did. Yesterday afternoon late. The man who answered understood the whole business. He said he wasn't the one who took the picture but that it had been given to him, and if I'd bring the money he'd hand over the negative and print. I wanted to do it then, but he said he was busy and that I should come around twelve or a little after. I told him that was awfully late but he said it was that or nothing— Well, he gave me the address and so I went right out there and asked the lady about him."

"What lady?"

"Oh—I forgot. The one who has the apartment opposite him. She told me his name was Austin and that she thought he worked for the *Express*. That's why I went there, why I was waiting when you saw me. I tried to phone him again later but he wasn't in that time either."

For a moment Casey forgot Austin and remembered only his admiration for this girl and her spirit and nerve. "And you went? With that little gun in your pocket?"

"What else could I do?" There was no answer to this and she continued. "But no one answered when I knocked and then I heard you coming up the stairs and—I guess you frightened me off. So I went back this morning. When I couldn't get in I thought he was out. That's why I got the janitor to let me in. I thought I could find the picture myself and not have to pay. And when I went in he—he was there on the floor."

Casey started to interrupt and thought better of it.

"I started to look. I made myself search the room. When I found the desk was locked I—I took his keys from his pocket."

Casey just stared at her.

"And I'm glad I did," she said, a sudden defiance in her tone. "Because I found them."

"Found what?"

"Pictures. A whole stack of them."

"Wait a minute." Just thinking of what this slip of a girl had done made Casey a little groggy. He felt as though someone had clipped him on the chin and that these things he was hearing were part of a dream. He went over to the table and poured a swallow of Scotch and downed it. "What kind of pictures?"

"All kinds. My brother's was there. There were a few more quite like it and others I didn't understand."

"What did you do with them?"

"I took them. I had them in my bag when you came. That's why I was so afraid."

"I'll be damned. I'll bet you'd have plugged me too."

"Yes, I think I would have," Nancy Jamison said.

Casey ran his fingers through his hair. He went over to the mantelpiece and propped an elbow there. He was thinking about Austin now and finding that he could not yet accept that black-mailing theory. There was still no proof but this girl's word. He found himself studying her aslant, weighing the things she had said. He liked her. Her personality did things to him. And yet—

"Where are those prints now?" he asked.

"In there." She pointed at the fireplace.

He looked down at the ashes, finding traces of paper ash among the lighter gray of the wood. "All of them?"

"All of them."

"What about the negative?"

"That's there too." She tipped her head and a frown bit into her forehead. "But that was the only one. There weren't any negatives for the other pictures. There was a print and a negative of my brother in an envelope, and there was an elastic around this and the other pictures, and when I looked through them I found another print of my brother."

"Just in case, huh?" Casey said disgustedly. "Holding out an extra print." And then he stared over her head, thinking about that stack of pictures she had mentioned, wondering about the negatives. Suppose they had not all been destroyed, those negatives? What about the pictures that didn't sell? Not even that racket was a hundred percenter—

Suddenly he straightened. He stared hard at the girl, not seeing her, but something else a long way off. Then he asked for the telephone, a snap in his voice.

Nancy Jamison eyed him curiously, pointing toward an inner hall. He went to a table there and asked for the *Express* number. When he was connected, he demanded the studio. "Hello," he said, when Tom Wade's voice came back to him.

"Hey," Wade said breezily. "Where are you? Logan's on his way down. Said he wanted to go over Austin's desk in case—"

"Austin's desk?" Casey yelled. He was squeezing the telephone now and his throat was hard and dry. "Are you alone? Then listen. There's a steel box in that desk. In the right-hand lower drawer. Get it out. . . . Yes, now. Put it in my desk. Shove it back behind something. . . . No, not there. That's where my bottle is. In another drawer. Go on now. Put it away. I'll hang on." He waited, realized his hand was sweaty and loosened his grip. When he heard Wade's voice again some of the stiffness went out of his neck.

"Okay," he said. "And get this. You've never seen that box. You don't know anything about it, or what he kept in his desk, or how the lock got broke. . . . Never mind. Just remember what I said . . . I'll call back." He hung up and went into the front room.

Nancy Jamison was standing by the fireplace now, a certain breathlessness in her voice as she spoke. "What is it?"

"I don't know," Casey said. "A hunch. Have you still got those keys?"

"Why—yes."

"I'd like to borrow them. I think it's about time I took my coat and hat too."

She was smiling a little when she came back with his things. She handed him the keys and he shrugged into his coat.

"Thanks," he said and saw she was offering her hand, and took it. "I still don't think you're right about Austin but I'm going to find out. And anyway, I had a nice time at your party."

She still held his hand. She looked right into his eyes and he could see how deep and clear and compelling were her own. "I'm glad you came," she said finally. "I like you." She walked with him to the door and held it open. "No matter what you find out, I hope you'll come again," she said.

CHAPTER FIFTEEN
THAT SICKLY FEELING

THERE WAS A RESTAURANT on the corner. It wasn't much of a restaurant, but it was a place to eat and there was a telephone booth by the cashier's desk. Casey went in and was waved to a table at the wall by a waiter.

He ordered Scotch and when the drink came, asked for chops and baked potatoes. He drank the Scotch slowly, glancing at the clock over the door. He kept thinking about the steel box in Perry Austin's desk, and Austin, and the things Nancy Jamison had told him. He kept telling himself she was wrong, yet all the time he knew how very real were the opportunities for blackmail among news-photographers.

The waiter came with the chops and Casey looked at the clock again and went into the telephone booth. He waited impatiently for his connection, a nervousness striking through him until he heard Wade's voice.

"Has he gone? What about the box?"

"It's okay," Wade said. "He wanted to know who busted the desk and I told him I didn't know. He said maybe it was the guys that busted yours. He searched hell out of it but he's gone."

"Good," said Casey, and relief flowed into the words.

"What's in it?"

"What's in what?"

"The box."

"How the hell do I know?" Casey said. "And listen. Keep your hands off it, understand? I'll see you later."

The marceled young man who sat behind the quarter-circle of desk in the dimly lighted lobby still smelled of hair tonic. He took one look at Casey, apparently remembered him from last night and, though his mouth bunched in distaste, said nothing. Casey stepped into the elevator. "Four, Sam," he said to the Negro operator. "Mrs. Endicott in?"

"Yes, sir," Sam said. "*Yes,* sir."

"Company?"

"No, sir. Least I don't think so, sir."

When Louise Endicott opened her apartment door, Casey was standing close. "Hello, Louise," he said, and moved in, slowly, but wedging himself in the opening so that she had to step back or get pushed.

"Just a minute," she said coldly.

By that time Casey was already in. He grinned at her. "You remember me, don't you?" he said, and walked past, leaving her to close the door. He waited for her at the entrance to the living-room.

She came up to him, eyeing him sullenly. She wore a black crepe dress. It had a high neckline but it wasn't especially modest because it was so tight and sleek around the waist and hips, and bias-cut above for extra room. He didn't think she wore a brassiere and decided she didn't need one.

"You've got a nerve," she said.

"You know I have." He glanced over the living-room and found it enormous. Most of the furniture was oversized; it had to be to keep the scale right. "This is what you had in mind when you used to go out with me, isn't it?"

"I only went out with you twice," she said.

"My, how things have changed."

"What do you want?"

"Five minutes of intimate conversation. And look." He let one lid come down and his grin was amused but sardonic. "We're alone. Just skip the grand manner and be yourself, will you? This is old Casey speaking."

She didn't want to smile but traces of it appeared in the corners of her eyes. She shrugged and Casey thought she did it well. "All right," she said, and went over to the divan.

"Was Bernie Dixon here last night?" he asked casually.

She blinked once. "What a question."

"Was he?"

"Well, really—" She drew herself up.

Casey sighed. "Listen," he said patiently. "You can't get haughty with Casey. I knew you when. I'm proud of you. You knew what you wanted and you got it. I'm sorry about your husband and I don't want to intrude upon your sorrow any more than I have to. All I want to know is—was Bernie Dixon here last night between eight and ten?"

"Does he say he was?"

"He says he was with a woman."

"Oh."

Casey sensed the change in her. She wasn't looking at him, but at something beyond, and now her eyes seemed very wise and thoughtful.

"Was it you?"

She gave a little laugh, a deprecating sound to indicate that such a thing was ridiculous. "Of course not."

"You know Harry Nye?"

"Y-e-s," she said, and suddenly her mouth was tight and straight.

"Know Perry Austin?"

"I've heard of him. I think I may have met him at the Berkely."

"Okay. Now was Dixon really here? And remember you can always deny it. All I want—"

"Excuse me." The door buzzer had interrupted Casey and Louise Endicott smiled and rose.

Casey rose with her, stared glumly at her symmetrical back and swinging hips. He walked across the room and came back. He heard the door close and then the voices, Louise's and a man's. He was too annoyed at the interruption to listen closely and presently they stopped. When he finally turned and saw Louise she was backing slowly into the room.

Something about the way she moved brought a sudden quickening of his pulse and he started toward her. Then he saw Nat Garrison and Garrison saw him. There was a gun in his hand.

"Well!" Garrison stopped, and a grin twisted his punch-scarred face. "Back up," he said to Louise. "Ain't this ducky?"

Louise Endicott stopped a few feet from Casey. Garrison looked from one to the other. He pointed the gun at Casey and his grin went away.

"You don't care what you do, do you?" Casey said.

"I want my dough," Garrison said.

"But I don't know anything about it," Louise protested.

"I'm telling you. I got five grand coming. I want it."

"Where do you think she's going to get it?" Casey said. "Out of her stocking?"

"Shut up, you," Garrison said. "I'll get you later." He paused but his scrambled mind could accommodate but one thought at a time and remained with the one that came last. "They're still look-ing for me," he said.

"Sure," Casey said. "Why don't you give yourself up and tell your story?" He heard Garrison make some reply, but only with his ears; his brain was thinking of other things. And the more he thought the more annoyed he became. Who did Garrison think he was, going around with that gun? You couldn't argue with him. You couldn't tell what he'd do. It was like talking to a half-wit. He was just as likely to start pulling the trigger as not.

Thinking of these things, Casey moved over to one end of a refectory table behind the divan. It had a tapestry runner on it and a vase in the center and two silver dishes. He leaned his weight stiff-armed on one end of the table and glowered at Garrison.

"She'll give you your dough if you've got it coming."

"You know she will—and I've got it coming."

"But she has to get it from the bank, don't she?"

"Shut up," Garrison said. "I'm gonna take care of you."

"That's swell."

"You're not gonna be around to put the finger on me."

Casey sneered at him. "Going to rub me out right here in front of another witness?"

Garrison thought it over. He came to the opposite end of the table. His face got more twisted and he apparently found this new question a tremendous problem. "I could rub you both out," he said.

"You don't care what you do with your dough, do you?"

"What dough?"

"The five grand you won't get if you rub Louise out."

"I know what I'm doin'," Garrison said. He wiggled the gun at Casey and put his other hand on the table, leaning on it and sticking out his chin.

"Sure you do," Casey said, keeping one eye on the gun.

"I'm gonna rub you out, that's what I'm gonna do. She ain't gonna talk."

He gestured toward the woman with the gun and Casey wrapped his fist in the tapestry runner and yanked hard. Garrison's stiff arm slid with the runner, jerking out from under him. He fell across the table on his face, the gun spinning from his other hand as the vase and dishes crashed to the floor.

Casey took two steps, and when Garrison cursed and pushed upright, hit him twice, a left and a right. Garrison may have been an iron man once, but that was a long time ago; then too, he'd never been hit by Casey. He went over backward and landed on his neck. Casey didn't even look at him. He picked up the gun and put it in his pocket. He was still sore. He picked up Garrison roughly and propped him in a chair.

"Just so I can watch him," he said. "Where's the phone?"

Louise Endicott let her breath come out and her breasts sagged. She fanned her face with one hand and the color crept back into her cheeks. "He scared hell out of me," she said. "I guess that calls for a drink— The phone's in there."

When Casey came back Louise Endicott had two highballs waiting, one of which was already half gone. She looked at Garrison. He hadn't moved. "What's his trouble?" she asked.

"Ahhh—" Casey took a swallow of his drink. "He's been smoking opium." He cocked an eye at her, studying her. "Was Bernie Dixon here last night between eight and ten?"

"There you go," Louise said. She'd lost her dignity now. She wasn't high-hat any more. She looked him over carefully and sighed. "All right," she said. "Because if you hadn't come I guess I'd have been even worse off. Yes, he was here. Only don't forget. I can retract that if—well, you know." She smiled up at him crookedly. "For the sake of my reputation."

"Um-um," Casey said dryly, and realized that for all his trouble he had no way of knowing whether she was telling the truth.

Jim Bishop looked Casey over for a full five seconds after he had opened the door before he said, "Hello, Flash. Come in."

"I just wanted to see if you'd crossed me off the list," Casey said.

Bishop shut the door. He waddled over to a walnut Capehart and turned down the volume. Casey glanced about. It was a small, cheap apartment, sparsely furnished with pieces that looked as though they had come from a second-hand store. All except the Capehart, which had probably cost more than all the rest of the furniture even when new.

"No," Bishop said. "I crossed you off for an hour this morning and then Lyda called back and I put you on again—in thirty-six point caps. Beer?"

Casey said he guessed not.

"How about one game of chess?" Bishop indicated an expensive-looking chess set that was laid out on a square table by the window, and looked hopeful.

"My game's rusty," Casey said. "And anyway I've got to get back. I just stopped in to tell you about the picture so you wouldn't—"

"Glad you did." Bishop was in shirt sleeves and slippers. He went over to a Morris chair which had been adjusted to an upright position so he could be sure to get out of it again. He lowered himself, grunting, sighed with relief. "And don't think we don't appreciate what you did," he said.

"She must have called Forrester after she called you last night," Casey said, and explained how Forrester and his two helpers had ganged up on him. He sat down on a chair arm and told what had happened to the print he had locked in his desk. "And then this morning," he said and spread his hands, "I was in the middle. All the way. That's why I don't like to hand out pictures. I couldn't tell the truth without giving you away."

"I know." Bishop looked at the floor and his voice was tired. "That's the hell of it. And it's not Lyda's fault, you know. I had to fight her plenty to make her agree to keep me out of it. It would've been all right except for that jail business. But for that, I guess it would be all right if Forrester and his crowd knew about me. I wouldn't embarrass the family. I'd keep low and nobody else'd have to know. But when you kill a man, when you're the kind of a fat slob that gets in barroom fights and hits a guy with a bottle—"

"Yeah," Casey said, and felt deeply sorry for this man who had become reconciled to spending the rest of his days alone and who thought so much of the happiness of his niece. "That was a bad break. Still, if you hadn't been plastered, if you'd known the guy and what you were doing, it would have been worse. You'd still be doing time. And you wouldn't have any Capehart, either."

He got up and put on his hat. "Well, I got to run, Jim— Sit still. I can let myself out."

Bishop nodded, his chins folding and unfolding. "I told Lyda last night we could count on you. And when she told me what happened this morning—well, I won't forget. Neither will she. We've kept the secret this long, and with this ticker of mine I'm living on borrowed time. The doc can't figure why it hasn't stopped long ago. I just want to be sure she marries the man she loves. I don't want anything to spoil it for her."

"Well, you don't need to worry about Logan," Casey said. "He's got the picture but he'll give it back."

Bishop told him to come again and play some chess and Casey went out and trudged down the stairs, feeling more weary and depressed than ever now that he had seen the man.

The keys in his pocket that Nancy Jamison had given him sent Casey back to the office. He found the studio deserted and was glad of that as he took the steel box from his desk. He found a key that would fit the lock and opened it. There was nothing in the box but a few papers and a bulky envelope. He opened this. It was full of films.

Afraid to look at them just then, he leaned back in his chair. He sat there quite a while, until he knew he could no longer postpone the issue. Then he began to go through them, holding them up to the light. It was difficult to tell about some of them but when he came to one that showed a man and a woman in a snug embrace he quit looking and put them all back in the envelope.

He knew he would have to print them, all of them. He would have to find out for sure, but he couldn't do it tonight. He could not force himself to the task now. He didn't want to think about it. Nancy Jamison had been right. Perry Austin was a blackmailer. That was enough for now. The pictures could wait. He put the envelope in an inside pocket. He opened the drawer of his desk and found his quart of bourbon more than half full. He put it into his topcoat pocket and reached for the telephone.

"If anybody wants me," he told the operator, "I'll be home. And I don't want to be bothered. . . . That's right. I don't feel good. I'm sick."

And as he hung up he thought, *You ain't kiddin' either, brother. You're sick.*

CHAPTER SIXTEEN

SILENCED FOR GOOD

CASEY HAD A SLIGHT HEADACHE when he awoke the next morning, and as he lay there wondering why he felt so low, he remembered about Perry Austin and that made the head worse. He sat up, decided he wasn't going to the right away, and got to his feet.

By a system of sliding black curtains, Casey had made part of the kitchen into a workable darkroom and as soon as he was dressed he got the envelope of Austin's and looked over the negatives. Almost immediately he was aware that they belonged in two classes. One was made up of originals; the other, he saw, consisted of copies—negatives which were simply pictures of other pictures. This was evident because the edges of the prints and the thumbtacks holding them to the easel were visible; but when these edges were masked out, a print could be made that, while not an exact duplicate, would compare favorably with the original.

This served only to increase his bitterness because it told him that not only had Austin been engaged in blackmail, but that even when he collected he took the precaution of keeping a copy, so that if conditions warranted he could follow up his victim and collect a second time. Therefore it would seem that all copies represented pictures which Austin had collected on; all originals indicated pictures which had not been sold at all because they had not been sufficiently dangerous, or because the victim was too tough to fall for blackmail.

Casey began to make prints of those negatives which were copies and had been sold. One was a close-up of a hotel registration card. The names on it meant nothing to him but the name of the hotel did: *The Butland*—rooms a buck and a half up and no questions asked. The next two were pictures of men and women he had never seen, ordinary pictures until you saw that the background was a nightclub entrance and realized how a jealous husband or wife might feel when confronted by this evidence. The fourth was another couple and this time Casey knew the man, not personally, but he'd seen him around. Clay Ackerman his name was, and he ran a large personal-loan company.

Right there Casey stopped. He was a tough man to convince, and a stubborn one. Everything he had seen said that Perry Austin was a blackmailer who used his connection with the *Express* to further his extortion efforts; yet even now Casey was not convinced. He was crazy, maybe, but he was going to find out for himself. He looked at the print again. Ackerman and some woman coming out of a doorway which bore the number 87. It meant nothing to Casey although it was obvious that the picture had been taken at night.

He slipped the print into the sink with the others and started to clean up while they washed. To hell with the rest of the negatives. He'd do them later. But first he was going to find out about Austin, and Ackerman was going to tell him.

The Citizen's Personal Finance Company had offices on the fourth floor of the Townsend Building. A cute little brunette at the information desk was twisting her mouth to one side and working on it with lipstick, but when she saw Casey she stopped to ask him what he wanted. He said he wanted to see Mr. Ackerman.

"I'll see if he's in," she said. "What was it you wanted to see him about? A loan?"

"No. A picture."

The brunette put down the vanity and lipstick, started to plug in a line. "I'm not sure—" she began.

"Just tell him a man's out here with a picture he ought to see."

She plugged in the jack, rang, and repeated what Casey had told her. She looked up at him presently. "What was the picture of?"

"Of Mr. Ackerman," Casey said. "And a woman, and a house that had number eighty-seven on the door."

The girl relayed the information, said, "Yes, Mr. Ackerman," and pulled out the jack. She picked up her vanity and smiled at Casey. "Mr. Ackerman will see you in just a moment."

Casey paced back and forth, looking through the glass partitions at the main office beyond. There were 30 or 40 people banging away at business machines, and one corner of the big room had been railed off to accommodate four desks and four smooth-looking gentlemen who sat behind them importantly, like vice-presidents of a bank. One was interviewing a customer. One was talking on the telephone. One stepped over and spoke to the fourth and the two of them got up.

Casey reached for a cigarette and sat down. Just after he'd got a light and an inhale the brunette called to him. Mr. Ackerman would see him.

"You can go this way," she said, and pointed to a door opening from the anteroom. "The last door on your right."

Casey thanked her and went along a narrow corridor to the designated door. He went in, finding himself in a large and beautifully appointed office that reminded him of Stanford Endicott's. At the far wall, behind an enormous desk, sat Ackerman. He was leaning back, smiling, a compactly built man with a pointed jaw and thick, graying hair. He had a cigarette holder, in one hand, a long black one. He put it in his mouth as Casey approached. "What about the picture?" he asked pleasantly.

Casey produced it and Ackerman sat up and reached under the desk. Somewhere behind him a door opened. Ackerman glanced at the picture and nodded.

A man walked past Casey to a door in one corner of the room. When he opened it Casey saw a landing and stairs going up and down. The man came back, a nicely-built fellow, young, clean-jawed, and blond. Ackerman leaned back in his chair and smiled. "All right, boys," he said.

Casey didn't get it. He scowled, started to speak. A hand fell on his shoulder, turning him. Not until then did he realize that when the blond man came in, three others came in with him. One of them took his arm, a black-browed fellow with big ears. Casey had never seen him before, but the other two were the vice-presidents he had seen talking outside.

"Let's go, bud," the black-browed man said.

"Wait a minute," Casey said. "What is this?"

"The bounce, bud."

Someone grabbed his other arm. They had him hemmed in now and he pushed one away so he could turn to speak over his shoulder to Ackerman.

"Listen," he argued. "This is no touch. I just want to—"

That was as far as he got. Somebody tried to yank him toward the door. He jerked back, pushing. The heel of a hand caught him under the chin, knocking his head back. He felt his legs being kicked out from under him and tried once more to call to Ackerman; then the hand was under his chin again and his hat went off and somebody clipped him in the stomach.

After that he got mad and things were vague. He remembered knocking the black-browed fellow on his haunches, of being dropped to one knee by a punch to the head; then he was knocking men down and they were getting up and slugging him and he was punching and watching them drop and backing up.

Finally something clipped him harder than usual and he felt his legs sag. When he got his eyes open he was on hands and knees and everything was quiet and nobody was hitting him any more. As though from a great distance he heard someone say, "Man, how you go!"

He shook his head and looked up. Ackerman was standing beside his desk grinning. "You had two of my boys on the floor and one in the air all the time you were in there. If Rusty hadn't tapped you with the sap I think you'd've taken the four of them."

He glanced toward the door through which Casey had entered. Casey, still on hands and knees, followed the glance. Blondy was holding a handkerchief to his nose; Black-Brows had a bloody mouth and a rapidly closing eye; the other two didn't look like vice-presidents any more.

"All right," Ackerman told them. "Get cleaned up. You'll be okay, Rusty, but the rest of you better call it a day. You'll give the place a black eye." He waved them out with the cigarette holder, put his hand under Casey's arm.

"I can make it," Casey said, and found he could. He felt his face. His teeth were all there but there was blood in his mouth and a lump on either side of his jaw. "Those were four nice gentle lads," he said morosely. "Where do you get 'em? Off of rock piles? Do they work here all the time?"

"They're in charge of complaints."

"And come all equipped with blackjacks, huh?"

"Only Rusty," Ackerman said. "We don't need one often, but you'd be surprised how people squawk." He had been getting a bottle and a glass from a cabinet as he spoke and now offered Casey a drink. "Wash your mouth out with that."

Casey tried it. His eyes widened and he sipped again incredulously. "Brandy!" he said, his lumps forgotten. "You don't get stuff like this any more," he said gratefully, and swallowed the rest of it.

"You know you don't. Help yourself." Ackerman was busying himself with an office icebox. He came back with some ice cubes. "You want to hold these on your face? Wrap them in your handkerchief— That's it. Sit down. I guess I made a mistake. When the operator told me about the picture I figured I'd have to chuck you out, but nobody can scrap like you and be a blackmailer— Who the hell are you, anyway? What's the beef?"

Casey sat down. The second brandy made him feel better. He wasn't even sore any more. He sort of liked this guy. "I work for the *Express,*" he said. "And never mind how I got the picture. I'm more afraid of it than you are. All I want to know is, did you pay? And who to?"

"Sure I paid," Ackerman said. "That was nearly a year ago. The wife and I were separating and if she got hold of that picture I'd've had to up the settlement. I gave the lad a grand and told him if he came back I'd throw him down the stairs. He handed over the negative and print and I thought that was that. I'm divorced now. The picture isn't worth a dime. So when you come in—" He shrugged. "I'm sorry as hell, but you see how it was."

"You don't know the fellow that collected?" Casey asked.

"There were two. The one that took the picture—I saw him when he did it—was not the fellow that collected. That one was tall, good-looking in a ratty sort of way, Mustache—"

"What kind?"

Ackerman thought it over. "Pointed. Slick. The other fellow was smaller. He had a mustache too, but little, clipped."

"That does it," Casey said bitterly, and began to feel bad all over again. He knew what the score was now. Austin took the pictures and Harry Nye did most of the collecting and framing.

"Does what?" Ackerman asked.

"Tells me all I want to know. Tear that thing up and throw it away. Forget it." He got up. "Sorry I bothered you, but it was worth the beating."

"Beating?" chuckled Ackerman. "You? Did you see my boys? Hell, you don't look bad. You might've bumped into a couple of doors. Why don't you have another slug of that brandy before you go?"

Lieutenant Logan was slouched low in his chair, his heels on the desk. He was staring morosely at his shoes when Casey came in the office, and he shifted his gaze without changing its quality or moving his head.

"Seen Harry Nye?" Casey asked.

"No. But we will."

Something in the inflection of Logan's voice interested Casey and he sat down, drawing up his chair. "Looking for him, are you?"

"Plenty. What happened to your face?"

"A bee stung me."

"Three times, huh?" Logan said. "Once on each side and once in the mouth." He swung his feet down, his gaze more curious now than morose. "Well, it's about time somebody gave you a working over— Who was it?"

"You wouldn't know him," Casey said. "It was about a picture."

"Okay then, what're you sore about?"

"I got trouble."

"*You've* got trouble?"

Casey watched Logan, saying nothing. Logan lit a cigarette, broke the match between thumb and finger. "What'd you want to see Nye about?"

"Just wanted to see him." Casey felt the bruises on his jaw and ran his tongue around the inside of his lips. It felt like an inner tube but he didn't think it showed much from the outside. "This Endicott business has got you down, huh?"

"And not only me, fella. This has really turned into something. Hot bonds, hell." He grunted sourly. "There's a cut-rate auto supply store down on Weber Street. Been there over a year. Advertised in the *Express*." He smoked silently and Casey waited. After a while the rest of it came out. "It's closed today. Cleaned out. There ain't even an old tire in the place."

The silence came again. Logan nursed it awhile.

"We found some records in Endicott's office. That's how we got wise. Nobody there—in the store, I mean. We located two clerks. They're all right. Didn't know a thing. The manager's gone and nobody knows where. Some guy came along and said they were closing up, handed the two clerks a week's pay, and told them to beat it."

"Today?"

"Yesterday."

"It wasn't Endicott. He was dead."

"You catch on quick," Logan said. "Endicott is rubbed out. Somebody's got to be in with him. Whoever it is knows the records will be found and then school will be out. Simple, huh?"

"The store was full of hot tires and accessories."

"Keep figuring. You're doing all right. That stuff was probably trucked in from every hijack job this side of the Mississippi. By now it's off the road. It's hot, again but it can be sold later."

"That's all right, isn't it?" Casey said. "No wonder Endicott was in the chips. Hot bonds, hot auto supplies—"

"In the chips. Hah!" Logan mashed out his cigarette. "We got an order to open his safe-deposit box. One of those big babies. It was full of cash. Guess how much?"

"How much do I get if I'm right?"

"Six hundred grand. Six hundred thousand dollars."

Casey leaned back and started to whistle. He stopped because it hurt his lip. He said, "That makes it sort of nice for Louise,"

"You know it. Especially when you figure he had talked about divorcing her."

Casey's brows came up. "Talked to whom?"

"Somebody in his office."

Casey sat there a minute, trying to assimilate all this information, but mostly thinking about Perry Austin and Harry Nye and what a stink it would make if the news of that blackmailing got around. He put on his hat and started to get up.

"Sit down," Logan said. "What's the matter? Am I boring you?"

"A little."

"I got more. Listen. There's wholesale jeweler in the Rand Building. Nice little guy. Of course he may wind up doing a couple of years the hard way, but a nice little guy."

"More records?"

"More records. We had a talk with him. He's got a legitimate business—or did have. Small, but okay. A couple of years ago somebody sells him a bill of goods. It's Endicott. He's got a nice story about wanting an outlet for refugee jewelry. Old stuff but good. All remodeled—so you can't tell where the hell it came from. The guy falls for it and makes a perfectly legitimate market for hot rocks, a natural outlet. He sent stuff out on consignment, like most of them do." Logan sat up, exasperation riding his words. "Why, damn it all! Yesterday, when a guy comes around and says he's going to withdraw this stuff from the wholesaler, there's a string of pearls over in Lyons & Son—the snootiest store in town. They had 'em in the window. The wholesaler calls the string back. He has to turn it over along with everything else that wasn't his own."

"Well, anyway," Casey said cheerfully, "you got the wholesaler. He didn't skip on you."

"Oh, swell," Logan groused. "Fine. He didn't skip because he had the shop and stock of his own. And anyway he thought everything was on the level. That's *his* story." He got up and went to the window, continued without turning around. "Last week a $200,000 jewel break in Miami. A month ago a $140,000 stick-up on Long Island. And you know where the loots ends up? In Lyons & Son's window."

"You got to admit it's a nice setup."

"Sure I admit it."

"And big."

"Six hundred thousand dollars' worth—and for a guy who probably only worked on commission. Hell, it's probably been going on for years."

"And if it hadn't been for this bond job—" Casey said, and then he thought of something else. "What about the guy that came around to close up the auto shop and paid off the clerks? The guy that told the wholesaler he wanted the stuff back?"

Logan turned, his tone sarcastic. "I wasn't sure you'd make it," he said. "But you did. Yes, sir, you did it all by yourself." He came over and tapped Casey's knee. "That's why we're looking for Harry Nye. What do you think of that?"

Casey looked at him. He didn't answer until he had a cigarette. Then he said, "I think you're nuts. Nye's not big enough to be behind a thing like that."

"Bernie Dixon is."

"I'm talking about Nye."

"Two guys saw him, the two clerks and the wholesaler—he's been contacting the wholesaler for a couple of months in place of Endicott—and the description they gave us fits Nye."

"He was only a runner then."

"So he's only a runner. I want him. He worked for Endicott. He hung around Dixon's Berkely. I think Dixon's our boy, but I'll take Nye for now."

"You think Dixon killed Endicott?"

"Till I find someone I like better."

Casey looked at his cigarette, thinking of the thing Louise Endicott had told him the night before. "Mrs. Endicott told me something last night," he said. "I didn't tell you."

Logan's face tightened and his eyes were narrow. "When did you ever tell me anything?"

"I'm going to tell you now, if you'll keep your yap shut long enough. What the hell is this, anyway?" Casey got up, his gaze sullen and hot. "Do I have to stay here and listen to all this crying?"

"Okay." Logan wasn't sore any more. He hadn't meant to be in the first place. It was just that the breaks were piling up on him and his temper was frayed. "Take it easy. What did she tell you?"

"She said Dixon was with her between eight and ten the night Endicott was murdered. While I was waiting up there with Garrison she told me. There's only a cook and a houseboy. She sent the house-boy out and the cook went home."

Logan sighed and sat down. He kicked the edge of the desk gently, moved his shoulders wearily. After a while he said, "She could be lying."

"She could," Casey said. "She said she might retract the statement later, anyway. I just thought I'd tell you."

"Thanks." Logan kicked some more and sucked his lips. "It could have been one of those hoods. He could have hired them. I've been figuring he did. They know their stuff, damn 'em. They haven't said ten words since we started to work on 'em." He looked up. "It could have been one of them."

"Maybe," said Casey, "but I think you're reaching now."

"With my fingernails," Logan said, and then the telephone rang. "Yeah, speaking. . . . What?" He sat up. "Where? Okay. . . . Yeah. Sure. Right away."

His voice was tired when he finished. He put the telephone down gently and his mouth curved in a grim smile. "Well, I knew we'd get a break," he said. "That's one thing about Logan. He always gets the breaks. I wanted him and I got him."

"Who?"

"Harry Nye."

Casey rose, hesitated, his eyes puzzled as he watched Logan reach for his hat and coat. "Now you're getting somewhere," he said finally.

"Sure am." Logan put on his hat.

"If you can only make him talk—"

"Nobody can do that. You have to find them alive to make them talk."

"Alive?" Casey said.

"He's downtown," Logan said. "In an alley. In his car. With a slug in his head. They tell me he's been there quite a while. Come on," he said, and opened the door and walked out.

CHAPTER SEVENTEEN
THE CANCELED CHECKS

THE STREET WHERE HARRY NYE'S coupé was parked was little more than an alley, but it carried considerable truck traffic in the daytime by virtue of its use as a loading outlet for the stores which backed up to it on either side. By the time Casey and Logan arrived, the area around the coupé was roped off and after one look at the reporters and photographers gathered about, Casey knew he was not going to get any exclusive pictures or information at the moment. If he'd had any hopes, Logan destroyed them.

"It's outside the ropes for you this time," he said, getting out of the car. "But stick around."

Casey knew what he meant. It was dangerous for the police to play favorites among members of the press—unless one of them had special information, which, in this case, Casey had not. He burrowed in among the others and spotted Tom Wade and Egan, a leg man from the *Express*.

"What do we know?" he asked.

"Nothing," Egan said. "Except he was shot once in the side of the head. The gun's in the car. It's been here all day, I heard some guy say."

Wade had his camera out. Casey produced his and opened it. He moved up against the rope and took a general shot of the immediate alley, the coupé, the dozen or so cops and plain-clothes men who milled about. The ambulance was already there and presently the body was carried out of the coupé. It wasn't a pretty sight. They couldn't straighten it out right and when they put it on the ground for a final inspection by the Examiner's man, Casey glanced about, ducked into a near-by doorway, found some back stairs and climbed them to a hall window. He got this open after a struggle and leaned out. It made a good picture, shooting down like that, and he took a second one as the stretcher was loaded into the ambulance.

"Why didn't I think of that?" Wade asked as Casey came back.

"You'll learn." He handed Wade the film holder. "Take this back when you go."

Wade looked at him with one eye. "What about you?"

"I'm sticking around," Casey said quietly. "By special dispensation. And don't crab it for me."

They waited a few minutes and finally Logan and Danaher, the precinct captain, came over and made a statement for the press. They said apparently Harry Nye had been killed late last night or early this morning; he'd been shot once through the side of the head at close range. Yes, the gun had been found on the seat. Suicide? A possibility. Was there any connection between Nye's death and the murder of Stanford Endicott? They could not say at this time.

A uniformed husky threaded through the knot of newspapermen and tugged on Casey's sleeve, giving him a wink and a jerk of the head as he did so. Casey edged away from the others. "The lieutenant says to meet him on the corner of Franklin."

"Okay," Casey said. "Thanks."

He closed his camera, put it in the plate case and slung it over his shoulder. He moved out of the alley without being noticed by the others and ten minutes later Logan and Manahan picked him up in the police sedan.

"Give," Casey said.

"Hah!" Logan's voice was bitter. He was staring straight ahead, his mouth a thin grim line. "Give, huh? Don't I wish I could. The only contact we have between the auto store and jewelry guy and Endicott—and somebody beats us to it."

"He got it last night?"

"The doc can only guess until he does a p.m. He figures between twelve and two but may change that later. How do you like that?" he asked. "Five thousand-seven hundred and twenty-nine trucks have passed that coupé since morning and he'd've been there yet if a driver hadn't tried to move the heap."

"What about the gun?"

"On a hunch the same one killed Endicott."

"Numbers?"

"Filed."

"But good," Manahan said, swinging the sedan into Washington and then up Bromfield. "He knew his stuff, whoever fixed it. Used a punch and hammered the metal down to destroy the molecule setup of the original numbers."

"Listen to him," Logan said. "An expert."

"All right," Manahan said, "but that's what he did."

"What about the one that killed Austin?" Casey asked.

"It was his own. Looks like the guy walked in with a gun. Austin tried to get his out, and the guy took it away from him and used it on him."

"You know when yet?"

"Between twelve and twelve-thirty."

Casey fell silent, trying to think of what he had been doing during that time. Suddenly he realized that it was then that he had knocked on Austin's door. And that girl, Nancy Jamison, had been there between 12:00 and 12:15. He was still sorting these things out in his mind when the car began to slow and he saw the entrance to the Club Berkely up ahead.

"You gonna give Dixon the business?"

"I'm going to try." Logan got out, stopped at the door as Casey lingered on the sidewalk. "What's the matter?" he said. "Don't you want to come in and kibitz? It might hand you a laugh, watching him give us the run-around."

"I have to make a couple calls," Casey said, watching Logan eye him narrowly. "I'll wait out here. If I miss you, I'll stop by your office."

Logan shrugged and pushed open the door. Casey waited, holding the door open and watching Logan speak to a man who was sweeping the foyer. When the two detectives continued across the main dining-room, Casey walked back to the street and flagged a cab.

Within ten minutes he was cruising down a wide, tree-lined street flanked by four- and five-story apartment houses which were moderately new, nicely cared for and representing the maximum of respectability—in an upper middle-class way. He left the taxi at the corner, walked rapidly down the street, glancing at numbers, and turned in at the third house.

In the vestibule he inspected the chromium-trimmed mailboxes, tried the inner door, found it unlocked and looked in the foyer, which proved to be an attractively appointed affair with two elevators and no desk clerk or telephone service. Then, turning back to the sidewalk, he hiked down the street until he came to a drugstore and a telephone booth.

"Hello," he said a minute later.

"Yes, please," replied a thin, high voice. "Mr. Dixon's residence."

"Are you the houseboy? What's your name?"

"Emanuel, sir."

"Well, listen to me, Emanuel, and don't make any mistakes." Casey's voice was hard and gruff. "This is Lieutenant Tasker at police headquarters. You alone?"

"Yes, sir."

"Well, get your hat and coat and come down here. I want to see you right away."

"But—Mr. Dixon. I should call Mr. Dixon—"

"Dixon is already down here, son. That's why we want you. Now are you coming down like I tell you or do you want me to send the wagon?"

"Oh, no, sir. I come. Emanuel come."

"And quick, like a goose, you hear?"

Casey ran to the corner, turned it and slowed down, taking the opposite side of the street. He hadn't gone 50 feet when a brown-skinned little man came running out of Dixon's apartment house and started down the street, coattails flying.

Casey said, "Nice going, Emanuel," and ambled idly across the pavement.

Bernie Dixon's apartment was on the top floor. Casey studied the lock a moment and then, though he had two bunches of keys— Perry Austin's and his own—he took out his pocket knife and slid the blade between the molding and the casing of the door. He pried gently, reached for a thin strip of celluloid he carried in his vest pocket, slid it along the crack until it came to the sloping surface of the bolt, pushing firmly until it slid back and the door popped open. He went in quickly, glanced up and down the hall, tapped the molding back although it did not really need it.

He got a shock when he saw what Bernie Dixon had done to the apartment. It wasn't so large—six rooms, and he went through them all because he wanted to know where the back door was in case he had to leave hurriedly—and probably did not rent for more than a $150 a month; but that was only for appearances. Inside there were Persian rugs and bits of sculpture done in teak and ebony, and at least 12 paintings that, even if you didn't know a thing about art, could not fail to impress. Casey even forgot himself long enough to make sure that one of them was a Bellows, another by Degas, a third, which he thought stank, by Picasso. He stopped looking then, figuring that if three were originals, all were authentic. He wished he knew how many thousands of dollars they represented.

There was an enormous break front opposite the fireplace and he went to it, examining the desk part and finding it locked. He got out the two bunches of keys, tried four of them before he got one that would work; then he pulled up a chair and sat down.

He did not know what he was looking for, hadn't the faintest idea, in fact. All he wanted to do was look around awhile and see if he could find anything at all that might show a connection between Dixon and Perry Austin, or Harry Nye, or even Stanford Endicott. It would only take one murder to convict Dixon—assuming that he was guilty—and Casey didn't care which it was. If he could find something that might help Logan, okay; if not, he at least had tried.

He started looking through the desk, not always conscious of just what he was handling since always in the back of his mind was the thought of Perry Austin. He did not know now whether the photographer had been killed as he had first thought—because of the film holder Casey had entrusted to him, or whether he had died because he had found something in Endicott's office and had then tried to blackmail the killer. Either way, Casey wanted to do something about it. Not that he felt he was any good as a detective but simply because, in this case, he happened to have a few facts that he had been unable to tell Logan. The important thing was that no one find out that Austin was a blackmailer; by helping out now, he might get co-operation later if Logan learned the truth.

He found nothing of interest in the desk part of the break front and tried the drawers beneath it. Presently he came across some used checkbooks. He took one out—it was of the three-checks-to-a-page variety—and leafed through it, glancing at the stubs until he came upon a name that stopped him.

The name was Adele Dixon. He said it over a couple of times as he turned the sheets and then, a little farther on, he saw the name again. The amount written on the stub was $1200. He looked back at the other stub and found the same figure.

Going through the book quickly he found that the name appeared five times in all, always for the same amount and with the dates approximately a month apart. He opened another drawer, pawed through it, opened a third. Here he found some envelopes containing canceled checks and said, "Hah!" softly and fingered through them until he found one made out to Adele Dixon. He turned it over, saw the stamp of the Traders' Trust Company, a New York City bank.

His dark eyes were remote and sleepy-looking as he put the check in his pocket. He didn't know what it meant, but it *could* mean something; it could mean a lot of things. He replaced the envelope and closed and locked the desk. He let himself out of the apartment cautiously and walked briskly down the street.

Logan and Manahan were just coming out of the Club Berkely when Casey got out of the taxi, and he could tell by the grim twist on the lieutenant's mouth that he had not accomplished very much in the past half-hour. They climbed in the police car without a word and not until Manahan had shifted into high did Casey speak.

"No dice?"

"Maybe, maybe not. We didn't expect to bust this thing by just talking to him. All I wanted was a line on him last night. We'll be back, maybe, when we find out when Nye got it. If we get a little more we'll get a warrant and start tearing into some of those files of his."

Casey handed him the check. Logan looked at it, swiveled his eyes at Casey, turned the check over and back again. "Who's Adele Dixon?"

"That's for you to find out."

"Where'd you get it?"

"What do you care?"

"I care plenty."

"Look," Casey said patiently. "I don't want to argue with you. If you want it, say so. If you don't, give it back. I happen to know Bernie Dixon's been writing one of those a month for a long time. I thought maybe you'd want to find out why."

Logan leaned back and gazed out the window at the midday traffic. After a half-minute of sightless inspection he said, "What good is it?"

Casey sighed and leaned back. "Night before last," he said wearily, "I give you two hoods from Jersey. Yesterday I give you Nat Garrison. Not because I'm smart, you understand, but because they won't leave me alone. Okay, you get 'em anyway. Now do I have to do all the thinking for the Bureau too?"

"Don't be so damn smart," Logan said, but he wasn't sore. He was thinking. After a while he said, "She could be his mother."

"Or his sister. Or his grandmother. She could be his wife, too. Or a New York girl friend." Casey crossed his legs, continued idly.

"If you called New York or got on the teletype, and if a New York dick went to the Traders' Trust, maybe they'd tell the dick where Adele lived, and maybe if the dick went to see—"

"Shut up," Logan said. "Let me be the detective for a while, will you?"

Manahan ran the car in behind headquarters. Logan made no move to get out, but watched Casey with narrow-lidded speculation. Presently a suggestion of a grin came and with it a look of grudging respect. "Maybe Dixon *wasn't* with Louise Endicott the other night between eight and ten. That what you're getting at?"

"It was just a thought," Casey said.

"You cased his apartment while we were at the Berkely."

"And that's against the law," Manahan said.

"Maybe you'd better give it back then," Casey said. "You're receiving stolen property."

Logan chuckled briefly but his voice was sober when he spoke. "We'll find out. If he's been paying regular it could be to the kind of a dame that might do us some good. If Mrs. Endicott's kind of sweet on Dixon, and if she don't know about this dame, and if Dixon *wasn't* with her—hell, what am I sitting around here talking to you lugs for?" He got out of the car and entered the building, walking fast.

CHAPTER EIGHTEEN

MOMENT WITH THE LADIES

THERE WAS AN ASSIGNMENT waiting for Casey when he got back to the studio, and it was late afternoon before he could return to his apartment and finish making prints of the negatives he had taken from Perry Austin's steel box.

When he had taken them from the drier, he made himself a drink and then went into the living-room. He built a small fire in the fireplace, sat down in front of it, and began to throw prints and negatives in the flames, watching the paper curl and blacken, hearing the negatives hiss at him. From the entire collection he saved but one negative and three prints.

The negative was a copy of an original and the subject was a man in uniform—a very befuddled young man by the looks of him—holding a negligee-clad girl on his lap, Nancy Jamison had stolen the original negative and print of her brother from Austin's desk, but a copy had been made beforehand and now Casey put the negative in an envelope, added the folded print, and pocketed it so that he could return it to the girl when he had time.

There remained now but two prints. He had noticed, while making the others, that the girl who appeared on Jamison's lap also appeared in another picture, in a similar pose, but on another man's lap. He had noticed that of the remaining pictures, only two were of this same general type. In each of these the same girl appeared, not the one who had posed with Jamison, but another. And since Casey guessed that it was these two women who had worked with Harry Nye and Austin, he had taken the negatives, masked off everything but the girls' heads and enlarged them so that what remained were grainy but sizable photographs of two faces.

Casey studied them as he finished his drink, brooding, knowing what he wanted to do. The important thing to him now was to wipe out completely all trace of this thing Perry Austin had been doing. Austin and Nye had known the truth and they were dead; the people whose pictures Casey had just destroyed might know but they wouldn't be telling; the killer probably knew, but Casey couldn't do anything about that just now. That left only the two women, and about them he thought he might be able to do something. He rolled the two photographs carefully and got his coat.

Jackie King was a softly rounded brunette in her middle twenties. She had big eyes and a small, oval face, and when she opened the door of her apartment and saw Casey standing there her eyes got bigger and her teeth flashed in a smile. "Why, Mr. Casey," she said.

"Can I come in?"

"You certainly can." She stood away from the door and closed it after him. "Well, how did you ever find out where I lived?"

Casey grinned at her. He glanced over the snug little apartment and decided it might be a nice place to spend an evening now and then—if a guy could get in.

"You know the Club Berkely?" he said.

Jackie smiled again because it was a gag question. She was the cigarette girl at the Berkely.

"Well," Casey said, "I went in there and asked Joe, the second bartender, if he knew where you lived. He said he didn't but maybe Bert did. 'Know where Jackie lives, Bert?' he said. 'No,' Bert said. 'Hey, Mike. You know where Jackie lives?'"

"All right," Jackie King laughed, "I get the general idea."

Casey smiled back at her a moment and then the smile went away and he took the two photographs from his pocket and unrolled them.

"I'm trying to check up on a couple of girls. I thought maybe you could help me, Jackie."

"I will if I can."

He glanced down at the pictures. One showed a blonde, the other a brunette. They hadn't posed or made up for a portrait and these enlargements didn't flatter them much. One, the blonde, was flashily pretty; both looked cheap and common.

Jackie King took them from him and he watched her face, seeing the quick recognition, the tightening of her mouth before she looked back at him.

"You—you're not mixed up with them are you, Mr. Casey?" she asked earnestly.

"You know them?"

She nodded. "I know who they are. Clippers. Both of them."

"I'm not mixed up with them," Casey said. "You know how they work?"

She said she didn't. "In any way they can, I guess."

"Where could I find them?"

"They used to work on Huntington." She mentioned a third rate night spot. "I don't know if they're still there."

"Could you find out? If you could get a line on where they lived—"

She rose, handing him the photographs. "You sit there," she said. "I'll see what I can do."

She went to the telephone and gave a number. Casey watched her, listening hopefully and then anxiously as she hung up and tried another call. Altogether she made four calls before she wrote something on a slip of paper and turned to him.

"I know where one of them lives," she said. "The blonde. Her name is Fay Borden." She named an address and he saw that she had it written down. "The other one is Aileen Rogers, but it looks as if she'd left town. I'm sorry."

"Sorry?" Casey rose and put the pictures away. "You're my pal." He took her arm as he went to the door. "The next time I get to the Club I'm going to buy you some wine—if you'll drink it with me."

"I might," Jackie King said. She stood in the door as he went out and her eyes were bright and smiling and said they liked him. "I might if it's late enough."

Fay Borden had rooms on the top floor of a remodeled brick house not far from Charles Street. When she opened the door and saw Casey standing there she tried to shut it in his face, but he saw it coming and put his shoulder in the crack and gently but steadily widened it. For a moment or two she fought that pressure, leaning her weight against the panel, but in the end she had to fall back. That made her mad.

"Listen, you!" she shrilled. "Who do you think you are? What do you want?"

He closed the door and leaned against it. His crooked grin was not amused now; neither were the eyes that studied her. She was dressed for the street and wore a thin silk dress and four-inch spikes and a fox cape. Her hair was very yellow, except near the roots, and needed a rinse. Her skin was yellowish, where it wasn't caked with make-up, and her greenish eyes were hard and suspicious and just a little scared.

"You can't push in here," she said. "I don't care who you are. I've got friends. You needn't think—"

"Okay," Casey said, and looked over the room. It was messy and smelled of cheap perfume and cigarettes. *What a dump*, he thought. And then, *I hope she rents it furnished*. "Okay," he said again. "I'm only here to do you a favor, sister. Recognize these?"

He offered the photographs but she couldn't pry her gaze from him right away, and accepted them automatically. She backed up. When he didn't attempt to follow, she glanced at the top picture. It was the one of Aileen Rogers.

"What about it?" she asked.

"Look at the other."

She did. And then back at him, her sticky-looking lashes flicking wide.

"Know where that was taken?"

"No."

"Think hard. You had a soldier boy. A lieutenant. You were sitting on his lap."

For a second or two she made a show of defiance. "If you're one of those vice-squad chiselers—" She couldn't finish it. "Where'd you get it?" she asked hollowly. "Where—where's the rest of it?"

"You got any money?"

That started her again. She was scared but she wasn't quitting. "What if I have?" she demanded. "Suppose I do go out with a soldier? What's wrong with that?"

Casey kept giving her that crooked humorless smile and it began to wear her down. "Harry Nye was in on that frame," he said. "And a guy named Perry Austin took the picture. Did you read about Perry Austin in the papers?"

A sudden pallor showed through the make-up and he saw her wet her lips. When she made no answer he continued. "Do you know what happened to Harry Nye last night? I'll tell you. They found him in an alley around noon."

"What do you want?" she asked finally.

"Where's Aileen?"

"In Philadelphia."

"For good?"

"I don't know. She went out on the road with a unit."

"You rent this place furnished?"

"Yes."

"How much money have you got?"

"A couple of hundred."

"That should be enough," Casey said. He went over to the door, opened it. Her wide, greenish eyes were puzzled and uncertain. "You know what I mean, don't you?" Casey added.

"That I should—"

"Two guys who were mixed up in that picture business have been knocked off in the last two days. Aileen's gone, so she's okay. That leaves you." He walked back and took the pictures from her limp fingers. He gave her a final glance and walked out.

He was halfway down the stairs when he heard the door open. She called down to him.

"But—who are you?"

He stopped and looked up. "Just a guy who dropped around to give you a tip and some advice: beat it while you can."

• • •

A colored maid opened the dressing-room door and Casey saw Lyda Hoyt at the table and went in. Her face lit up at once and she held out her hand, bringing him to her. "I'm so glad you came," she said.

"I thought I might not get another chance," Casey said, feeling again her warmth and personal magnetism. "You close tomorrow, don't you?"

She said they did. That she was going to Hollywood for a picture. There was a chessboard on the table and he could see that a game was in progress, but apparently not for very long, since only four players had been removed—three pawns and a miter-headed bishop.

"I didn't mean to break up your game," he said.

"It doesn't matter. I try to get a game in before a performance. It—helps me to relax." She smiled. "But tonight I can relax with you. Sit down." She waved him to a chaise longue. "Over there."

"All right, Anna," she said. Anna went out and Lyda got up for cigarettes, holding a light for him. "Now," she said. "I want you to know how grateful I am for what you did."

Casey looked uncomfortable. "It wasn't much," he said. "Only for a while you had me in a spot. You called Forrester that night, and he came around for the picture and I couldn't tell him—"

"I know. It *was* stupid of me. But I was terrified. I really was."

"Sure," Casey said. "I chased you out of Endicott's office." He grinned. "You put that chair in front of me and I fell on my face."

"Did you?" Her eyes flashed their smile again. "I'm sorry."

Casey blew smoke at the ceiling. "I stopped in to see Jim last night," he said. "I wanted to be sure he knew how Logan got that extra print."

Her face sobered and she examined the tip of her cigarette. "I wonder," she said slowly. "I wonder if we're doing the right thing. Trying to keep it all a secret."

GEORGE HARMON COXE

Casey studied her. "You mean about your uncle?"

"My uncle?" She hesitated and returned to her regard of the cigarette. "Yes. I wonder what would have happened if Grant had found out."

"Jim wouldn't like it, would he?"

"No. When I told him I was going to announce my engagement he made me promise never to let Grant know. He—he said he'd kill himself rather than have it come out that—we were related—that there was a jailbird, that's what he said, in the family."

Her eyes were deeply troubled now and Casey couldn't think of much to say.

"I don't know," he said finally. "I think I'd let it ride if I were you. Jim's happy. Why not let well enough alone? If he knows you're happy he's glad because he can know he hasn't spoiled anything for you. If you fool around, if something should happen he'd be sure to think it was his fault—"

"I'm sorry." Lyda Hoyt rose and smiled wistfully. "I didn't mean to get so involved."

Casey got up with her and looked at the traveling-clock, realizing he'd have to go. He told her so.

"Yes, I suppose so," she said, glancing at the clock. She held out her hand and pressed his firmly. "You're right, of course. About Jim, I mean. It's just that I feel such a beast sometimes."

"I don't think you should," Casey said. "Well—"

She opened the door. "All right, Anna," she said and then, to Casey: "Good-by, Mr. Casey. I'll not forget your kindness—ever. And I'm sorry I've made you so much trouble."

"Nosey guys like me have to expect trouble," he said, and found his throat a little thick. "Good-by. I hope you'll be very happy."

CHAPTER NINETEEN

A FINE MORNING'S WORK

WHEN CASEY STOPPED IN LOGAN'S OFFICE the following morning on the way to work, he found the young lieutenant just putting on his coat.

"Ah, my friend," he said. "And how are you this bright and cheerful morning?"

Casey blinked and dropped on the nearest chair. He screwed his brows down and eyed Logan aslant. When the lieutenant began to arrange things on his desk to the accompaniment of a soft whistle Casey gave up.

"What is this?" he said. "You been eating those vitamin pills?"

"It is a bright and cheerful morning, isn't it?"

"Maybe you got this case all wrapped up," Casey said.

That stopped the whistling. Logan looked at him. "There you go," he said. "Always belittling."

"Give out," said Casey. "And where are you going?"

"I thought I'd call on Mrs. Stanford Endicott shortly."

"Oh-oh." Casey grinned. "So that check I gave you was something."

"It was indeed."

Casey sighed. "Now wait," he said. "Relax. Quit talking like Philo Vance. This is old Casey, the guy that gave you the lead. Keep it simple and unaffected."

"Okay," he said finally. "In this business a lot of things can happen in a very short time—thank God—and some of the leg work we've been doing is starting to shape up. First, Nye was killed—according to the M.E.—between one and two o'clock the night before last. By the same gun that killed Endicott. And while we're sweating our ears off trying to break an alibi Bernie Dixon said he had, a little old guy by the name of Cafferty who has been walking himself bowlegged for thirty years out of the Milk Street station comes up with the crusher.

"Cafferty, now, is a good cop. Dumb, you understand, but reliable. He's standing on a corner holding up the side of a building around 1:05. He's sure of the time because he called in at one—which is a break for us—and this was about five minutes later. All right. He's standing there when he hears a car take the corner pretty fast. The tires are squealing and that wakes him up. He lets the building stand there by itself and steps to the curb, and the street light gives him a gander at the car and who's in it. Guess who?"

"Dixon."

"And Harry Nye."

Casey grunted. "Dixon's lawyer'll have something to say about Mr. Cafferty's eyesight before he gets through and don't you think he won't. Night. Two guys in a coupé—"

"Okay," Logan cut in. "But he got the number. He identified the car and he'll swear that Dixon was the passenger because he was riding on that side. He says the driver was Nye, but he won't swear to it. But Dixon. Listen, when an old-timer like this Cafferty makes up his mind he's seen something, you can keep him on the stand four weeks and you'll always get the same answer. That's why they call us stubborn cops."

"It ain't enough," Casey said.

"Nye had a secretary," Logan said, as though he had not heard. "Name of Taber. Florence Taber. She phoned me yesterday afternoon after she'd read about what happened in the papers. She phoned me from the Statler."

Logan put on his hat, adjusted the angle of the brim carefully. "Nye had called this Taber up the night he was killed. He said he wanted her to get a room at a hotel—she lived alone—and stay there until she heard from him. He said he had to see Bernie Dixon and there might be some trouble and that's why he wanted her out of the way. If anything happened she was to get in touch with me—She did."

"That all she knows?"

"That's almost enough. Nye was scared. He had to see Dixon but he figured he was safe since he'd have the girl as an ace. If Dixon got tough, he'd tell him that he'd already tipped off the girl as to who he was going to see, figuring that would make Dixon lay off." He shrugged. "Whether he didn't get a chance to tell Dixon, or whether he told him and Dixon thought he was bluffing—or didn't give a damn—we don't know."

"Um," Casey said. "Or else Nye told him to lay off or the girl would go to the police, and Dixon killed him, figuring he would go to the girl and see that she kept her mouth shut—and then he couldn't find her, not knowing Nye'd told her to hide out— Not bad. It don't prove anything but—"

"It does to me," Logan said. "Let's go see Mrs. Endicott."

The Filipino boy who opened the door of the Endicott apartment told them Mrs. Endicott was not up yet and tried to convince them that he dared not disturb her. Logan pushed in, saying he was of the police. "Just tell her Lieutenant Logan is here," he said. "Tell her I have to see her. I'll wait."

They went into the living-room and sat down. Logan was impressed. He looked carefully about him, lit a cigarette, and leaned luxuriously back in his chair. "Not bad," he said. "A guy could have a lot of fun in a place like this."

They had to wait about a half-hour before Louise Endicott appeared. She was wearing a long black house coat with a sort of train and Grecian lines. It went well with her full-blown blondness. She would have been beautiful if it hadn't been for the annoyance in her eyes and the sullen droop of her painted lips.

"Good morning," Logan said cheerfully as he and Casey rose. "I'm sorry to disturb you but—"

"What is it you want?" Louise Endicott cut in, sitting down on the divan.

"Casey tells me that you were with Mr. Dixon at the time your husband was killed," Logan said.

"Really?" Louise gave Casey an icy stare. "I don't remember."

"That would be between eight and ten—eight-thirty and nine actually. Casey says you sent the houseboy out at eight."

"I told Mr. Casey not to quote me," Louise Endicott said. "I'm afraid I don't remember anything about it."

"We've been going through some of the records in Harry Nye's office." Logan was still polite, unconcerned. "There were some carbon copies of reports he had made about you."

Casey sat up. Louise Endicott leaned back and looked bored.

"You and Mr. Endicott were on the verge of separating, weren't you?" Logan asked.

"I don't see how that concerns you," Louise Endicott said. "As a matter of fact if those charges against him were true, if he was sent to prison for receiving stolen bonds, I should have divorced him in any case."

"These reports," Logan said, "were made to your husband. They concerned the movements of yourself and Mr. Dixon. They indicate that your husband was suspicious of you and that he had evidence enough to sue on his own account. Of course this happened before he was arrested."

Louise Endicott yawned to show she wasn't interested. Logan reached in his pocket and brought out two slips of paper. "Do you know anyone named Adele Dixon?"

"No."

"No? Then you didn't know that Mr. Dixon has been paying her twelve hundred a month for the past several years?"

Louise Endicott stared at him. She wasn't thinking about yawning now; her blue eyes were bright and narrow as they watched Logan move up to her and hand her the slips of paper.

"Those are photostatic copies of one of his checks," he said. "Front and back. We checked with the Traders' Trust and then with Adele Dixon to find out what the relationship was."

He held his hand out for the photostats. He went to his chair and sat down again, eyeing Louise Endicott steadily, saying nothing.

Casey watched him; he liked to see Logan work, when it was on somebody else. After a while he said, "Mr. Endicott was going to divorce you—until he got himself in a jam. And then you say you were going to divorce him. But you didn't figure on marrying Bernie Dixon, did you?"

Louise Endicott's face stiffened inch by inch and little by little the color seeped away.

"I guess he told you he couldn't marry you. He told you he was already married and—"

"That's a lie!"

"He's been married to Adele Dixon for ten years," Logan said. "She wouldn't divorce him and— I don't know, I'm only guessing, but I guess he could have divorced her on grounds of desertion if he'd wanted to—or maybe he couldn't."

"I don't believe it."

"About Adele Dixon? Why, that came straight from New York, Mrs. Endicott. I got that in black and white. She was his wife. Is his wife. And he was playing you for a sucker. He had no intention of marrying you. He was going to stall you until he got tired of the arrangement and then—"

"You're a dirty liar!" Louise Endicott jumped up. The house coat fell open to show a pink thigh and she flipped it about her angrily. She grabbed a cigarette from a box, tapped it so hard it broke. She threw it in the fireplace and took another. She got a light and sat down again, her color high, jaw rigid.

Logan gave her a few more seconds of silence; then he said, innocently, "No, Mrs. Endicott. Why should I lie to you? I thought I was doing you a favor. I thought this was something you ought to know." He hesitated and Casey watched in admiration. He was good, Logan was. When he continued his tone was almost hurt, it was so patient. "I just wanted to show you you were making a mistake about Dixon. I have his wife's address here, and her phone number. You can call her in New York if you don't believe me." He started to reach in his pocket.

"Never mind," Louise Endicott said. She was tapping one foot, hugging her breasts, her face tight.

Logan's lean face relaxed. He leaned back in his chair. "You'll only get yourself in trouble, trying to protect him," he said. "There's such a thing as perjury, even for a good-looking woman like you. Bernie Dixon wasn't here the other night between eight and ten—"

"No, he wasn't," Louise said.

Logan continued instantly: "But you sent the house-boy away?"

"Yes. Because Bernie phoned and asked me to. He got here just after eight and said something had come up and he couldn't stay after all."

"He went right out again?"

"Yes. And then he phoned later and said Stanford had been killed and it might look bad for him and that he might have to say he was here for an hour or so. He said he wouldn't offer the alibi unless he absolutely had to."

"Did you ever think he killed your husband?"

"Why"—the woman's eyes went wide and her surprise seemed genuine—"no."

"What did Dixon say about it?"

"He said it must be the ones who were mixed up in that—that bond business with him. They were afraid he'd talk. He said he knew how it might look—I mean, people might find out we'd been—friendly—and so he might need an alibi."

"I see," Logan said. He stood up. "Just one thing more, Mrs. Endicott. Did your husband accuse you of any, ah, intimacy with Dixon? Did he let you know he suspected anything?"

She looked at him a moment, then lowered her lashes. "Yes. He said he'd had this man, Nye, watching me."

"Thank you." Logan said. "Thank you very much."

Louise Endicott watched him move to the door with Casey, finally called, "But you don't think—"

"We don't know," Logan said. "We may have to ask you to make a statement later. If I were you I shouldn't mention this to Dixon. You've been his sucker long enough."

When they got out in the hall, Casey said, "Was that nice?"

"I just wanted to leave her in the right frame of mind," Logan said. "That is what I call a fine morning's work."

"You were lucky," Casey said, as they got in the car.

"Plenty lucky. It was that check. If Adele had been Dixon's mother or something I couldn't have got to first base. I still needed luck but I figured if Louise *didn't* know he was married—" He broke off, continued thoughtfully. "I think I've got the setup, now," he said. "I can't prove it yet, but things fit. See if this makes sense. Endicott and Dixon are in this business of peddling stolen property—of all kinds. Back of them are the mobs that do the work, but they're independent outfits spread all over the East and we can't help that now. All right. Dixon is probably the guy with the contacts and Endicott is the business man. Nye is probably in it too, but only like you said—a runner."

"He worked for both of them?"

"Endicott, I think. He may have known about Dixon, and after Endicott was knocked off we know Nye contacted the auto store and jewelry guy, so that time he was under orders from Dixon. But up to then I think he was Endicott's man, otherwise he wouldn't have made those reports about Dixon and Mrs. Endicott. Anyway, we start with Endicott getting nabbed for the hot bonds. I don't know if you know it, but the D.A. had him cold on that charge. They got him with his pants down and he knew it."

"So?"

"So he's got two angles. Fight the case and lose and take the big rap, or cop a plea and get maybe a couple of years. Now follow me. He's got six hundred grand in a vault. He's mad at his wife and Dixon and he's got proof, through Nye, that they've been two-timing him. He knows he's got to take the rap some way. Which way would he do it, assuming these angles of mine are right?"

"He'd sing," Casey said. "He has to do time so he takes the two years. He put Dixon on the spot to get even."

"Right. With Endicott turning State's evidence, Dixon would wind up with plenty years. What better way to get even with him for playing around with his wife? Especially when Endicott does himself all the good? He gets a light sentence. He's got plenty of jack in the vault when he finishes it. His wife doesn't know it and she'll probably divorce him and that won't cost him anything much."

"I'll buy that," Casey said.

"You know you will." Logan grunted softly and stretched his legs. "Endicott made one bad mistake. He was so sore at Dixon and his wife that he told Dixon what he was going to do. When I don't know. I don't know if Dixon went to the office to kill him or just went and was told off and shot him then and there. Anyway it was his only chance. Endicott wasn't kidding. Dixon would take a good stiff rap and he knew it. I figure if this cluck Garrison is telling the truth, that Dixon and Endicott were going at it when Garrison came. Dixon stepped into the next room and when Garrison beat it, he pumped two into Endicott's vest."

"And Austin and I damn near walked in on him. Boy, wouldn't that have been something?" Casey thought it over and gradually digressed to something else. "And Austin?" he asked.

"Probably like you said," Logan replied. "You got the pictures of Dixon. He sent those two hoods he'd been hiding to the office and they tailed you. Dixon knew Austin was with you. When the hoods didn't get the right plates from the case they swiped, and when they couldn't find it in your desk, they phoned Dixon. He either rubbed Austin out or they did. Anyway, they stole the film, didn't they? It wasn't at Austin's place."

Casey thought it over, and decided to let it ride. Logan didn't know that he had since got that film holder from Finell. But the theory was still reasonable. Austin might have been killed because the killer believed that he had the holder. Either that or the thing Casey was afraid of—Austin found something in Endicott's office that incriminated the killer and tried to make a deal. Well, it didn't matter. Logan didn't know Austin was a blackmailer; he wasn't going to know.

"What about Nye?" he asked. "You think he knew Dixon was the killer?"

"Could be. Doesn't have to be that, though. Nye was the only guy around that could still send Dixon to the pen for the other business. Nye knew about the auto store and the jeweler. If Dixon sent him around to get those guys out of town, and if Nye wanted to talk— Hell, he had plenty of reason to put Nye away." He sighed. "I only wish I could've got to Nye first."

"What're you going to do?"

"Talk it over with the Inspector. If it's okay we'll pick up Dixon on suspicion of murder—we can hold him twenty-four hours anyway—and get a warrant and go over his office and home. He's our boy."

CHAPTER TWENTY
FRONT-PAGE TRAP

BY 11.30 THAT MORNING the word had gone out to all precincts to pick up Bernie Dixon, and by one o'clock it became apparent that Mr. Dixon was not to be found. At 1:30 Casey telephoned Logan and was informed that it looked very much as if Dixon had gone into hiding temporarily, and at 2:00, Casey and Logan were in the office of MacGrath, the managing editor.

"All right," MacGrath said, swiveling his half-smoked cigar to the opposite corner of his mouth. "What's on your mind, Flash?"

Casey indicated the telephone. "Tell the girl you don't want to be bothered for fifteen minutes."

MacGrath eyed him curiously a moment, but when Casey stared back at him, he gave the necessary order. He looked at Logan. "What's this all about?"

Logan shook his head impatiently. "I don't know. I wouldn't have come at all only—" He sighed and glanced at Casey. "When he gets mysterious like this, sometimes he comes up with an idea. I could use one. Any kind of an idea."

"You think Dixon's holed up?" Casey asked.

"Hell, yes."

"What're your chances of finding him?"

"Damn small. A guy with his dough and his contacts could lay low for months. He probably wants to find out what the score is. If he finds out we got a case he'll stay low until he gets Nye's secretary and that cop, Cafferty, taken care of. If he thinks we haven't, he'll give himself up. We'll never nail him for the Endicott job or the Austin one. But the Nye thing is different. We got a couple other little things now. We've got a chance on that one."

Casey took a photograph from his pocket, unrolled it, and laid it on the desk. It was the picture he had taken that first night of the killer in the car, the one he had got from Finell's coat pocket.

Logan took one look at it and his neck bulged with anger. "Why, damn you!" he snarled.

"What is it?" MacGrath asked.

"You had it all the time," Logan said.

"No." Casey shook his head. "What I told you was right—at the time. It's the shot I took after the first murder." He told Logan the same story he had told MacGrath earlier, and then went on to explain what had happened to the film holder and how he eventually got it back from Finell.

MacGrath took the cigar from his mouth and squinted both eyes. "I've been thinking about that since you told me," he said. "Austin never had that picture—except to bring it here and give it to Finell. He was murdered for nothing."

Casey did not deny this, but it wasn't what he thought. It wasn't his opinion at all. All that morning he had been sitting in the studio, brooding.

There was a great loyalty in Casey, not only to the *Express*, but to his profession. He had been a photographer a long time and for all his crabbing and profanity, his clashes with Blaine, his grumbling over the injustices he suffered, he would not have changed jobs with the President. He could never have explained why, of course, because almost everything seemed to be on the debit side of the ledger. Backbreaking work much of the time and often routine, it meant being out in all kinds of weather, crawling out of bed in the middle of the night; it meant lugging a plate case wherever you went and taking chances that even reporters did not have to take.

That's how it was. Day after day. Picturing the contemporary drama of life but never thinking of it that way; thinking of it only as a job you liked and always knowing one thing: if you got a picture no one could ever deny it. Stories could be faked but to get a picture you had to be there. There was no glory, other than this, but there was a kick in walking up to Blaine's desk once in a while when he had a tough assignment and everyone thought it couldn't be done— a kick in walking up and slapping down that picture and saying, "What the hell do you care how I got it? This is it, isn't it?"

He'd watched the others while he had been sitting there brooding and he knew they all felt the same way. O'Hearn, tough, dependable, a veteran at 30; Klous, the sports man for 20 years, who made $50 a week and was sending his daughter through college; Wade, cocky and irrepressible; Finell, Naherny, Potchek, and Austin—

Always now there was that faint nausea in his stomach when Casey thought about Austin. He didn't want these other men who had worked with him to know; he didn't even want MacGrath to know. What had MacGrath said? That Austin wasn't his kind of man? How well MacGrath had sized him up. But no one was going to know the truth; no one was going to point a finger at the *Express* or its photographers and say they'd worked with a blackmailer. Casey was pretty sure now that Austin had not been killed because of that picture which now lay on MacGrath's desk. He had no proof, but he was convinced that Austin had found something in Endicott's office and had been killed by Dixon because of it. He looked at MacGrath and answered his statement, not believing what he said but making it sound convincing.

"How was he murdered for nothing? Once the killer had made his move, he had to put Austin away. He'd committed himself, hadn't he? He'd made the threat to get the film holder. Austin said he didn't have it. Would Dixon believe him? Whether he did or not, Dixon was cornered. What could he do? Shove the gun in his pocket and say he was sorry? He'd made his move and he was stuck with it."

He watched Logan as he finished to see if the explanation was going over, but he could find no clue in the lean, sober face. MacGrath cleared his throat. "All right," he said. "What're you getting at? What're we here for?"

"I think I can get Dixon," Casey said.

Logan said, "Nuts," and looked annoyed.

"Dixon—if your theory is right—hired those two hoods to put me away the night Endicott was killed," Casey said evenly. "Why? Because he recognized me on the street, thought I may have recognized him, and knew I took a picture."

"So what?" Logan said.

"Why hasn't he tried to put me away since? It's over two days now."

Logan tilted his head and frowned. MacGrath spoke quietly. "Because nothing happened."

"Sure," Casey said. "He has to figure I didn't recognize him or I'd have spilled it to Logan. He has to figure that either the picture was no good or something happened to it."

"So?" Logan said.

"So now we're going to let him find out different."

"That thing"—Logan tapped the photograph—"isn't worth a damn."

"But Dixon doesn't know it. He doesn't know what's on that film because he never got his hands on it."

MacGrath leaned back and chewed his cigar. Presently he looked down his nose at Casey. "You're a big guy, Flash. You'd make a good target."

Casey grinned because he knew MacGrath was way ahead of him; MacGrath was that kind. Logan was still struggling.

"Can I get in on this?" he asked.

"The afternoon sheets are carrying the story that you're looking for Dixon, that you want him for questioning. The city editions will carry something more." He looked at MacGrath. "You can get the word around—if Logan can't. Get over the idea that a new witness has been found in connection with the murder of Endicott, new evidence has come to light—I don't know how you're going to word it, but just get the story out and make it look like there can only be one answer to Dixon. You can say it's evidence that has been withheld by a local newspaperman. He'll know who you're talking about."

"You're crazy," Logan said.

"You think he won't?"

"Sure he will. He'll figure you had the picture all the time but were afraid to produce it. And then he'll come looking for you because the picture won't be worth a damn—I mean even if it was a good one—without your testimony. All the picture—the picture Dixon *thinks* you got—would show is him in a car at night. Not worth a damn. Because it doesn't prove when it was taken or where."

"That's what I'm telling you," Casey said. "That's why I told you I could give you Dixon. He's got to come looking for me."

"He could send somebody else."

"I doubt it. You don't pick up guys for that kind of a job in this town very often. He had two from Jersey and you got them. He did the Nye job himself, didn't he? He'll tackle me the same way."

"No dice," MacGrath said. "No. It's too risky. Why should you stick out your neck?"

Casey told his lie deliberately and convincingly. "Because it's my fault Austin's dead. If I'd had that film holder in my plate case when those hoods stole it from Logan's car, Austin would still be alive."

"That still doesn't make it your fault. You didn't know that." MacGrath threw his cigar away. "No," he said, and they argued some more.

But not for long. Logan was half convinced before they started, because Logan was a cop and he knew Casey made sense, that the plan presented the only chance he had of getting his man. "We'll keep someone with you from now on," he said.

"Like hell you will," Casey said. "And tip our mit that we're waiting for him? He won't try it on the street, anyway. He'll probably try to get me in my rooms."

"All right," Logan said. "We can fix that. Give me a couple of hours to get a telephone or two put in. You got a gun?"

"Several."

"Okay."

"No." MacGrath slapped the desk. "Damned if I'll let you take that chance."

Casey stood up. He leaned stiff-armed over the desk.

"You're always yelling about pictures."

"No."

"You'll get pictures if this works. You'll get an exclusive story." His smile remained, watching the reflection of MacGrath's struggle on his face. "Come on, humor me. You and Logan think up that story." He glanced at his watch. "It ought to be on the street by four-thirty, hadn't it?"

He went out before MacGrath could think of an answer.

Nancy Jamison had on slacks and a dirty, paint-smeared smock. Her pert young face was free of makeup and smudged on one cheek and the tip of her nose.

"Hy," she said cheerfully.

"Am I disturbing genius?" Casey asked.

"Genius welcomes the interruption." She waved him to a chair and he saw the canvas she was working on and her still-life group posed on the table. He cocked his head at the painting.

"Horrible, isn't it?" she said, looking for cigarettes.

"It won't be when it's done."

She drew a stool over to his chair and sat down, hugging her knees and brushing the lock of hair back again. There were a lot of things Casey wanted to say as he looked down into the warmth and friendliness in her hazel eyes, but he couldn't seem to get started, so he took out the envelope he'd been carrying since the day before.

"I've got a present."

"Oh—how nice." She opened the envelope and took out the negative and print of her brother. Her smile went away then and her eyes were troubled. "Where did you get them?"

Casey told her about Austin's steel box and the negatives.

"But I got one negative and a print from his desk."

"Yes," Casey said. "You got the original. But from that print he made this negative and this print. Just in case."

"Oh. You mean he might have tried to—get more money?" Casey did not answer her and presently she reached behind her and found matches and an ash tray on a coffee table. She burned the picture and dropped the negative in the flames. "Thank you," she said.

He said it wasn't anything, and she looked up at him, for several seconds, steadily, searching his face. "You're bitter, aren't you?" she said.

"Bitter?"

"About this Perry Austin. He worked with you. You feel it keenly, the things he did."

"Yeah," Casey said finally. "I guess I do. We've got seven cameras on the paper and any one of them could have the same opportunity. Most of them make less than Austin did, but you couldn't buy a picture from them, nor pay them to hold out one."

"Did anyone ever tell you what a grand person you are?"

Casey blinked and then began to blush. "Who?" he said defensively.

"You," Nancy Jamison laughed.

"Ahh—"

She jumped up. "Would you like a drink?"

Casey said he would, relieved at the digression. He said he was dying for a drink, and while she was gone a thing that had been in the back of his mind a long time burrowed to the surface and began to irritate him anew. It came from a thing Finell had said—that Perry Austin had come back to the studio that night and done some work with the copying camera. Those films, whatever they were, must have been in Austin's plate case, since he had not developed them at the studio. He had also taken a few pictures at the Club Berkely. Yet none of these film holders had been in that plate case when Casey had found him dead the following morning.

At the time, believing that Austin had been murdered because of the film holder containing the picture of Dixon in the car, Casey had assumed that the killer had taken all of those exposed film holders. However, if Dixon had not killed Austin for that, but for some other reason—

He got up as Nancy Jamison came back with his drink. When he had thanked her he said, "Do you know what a film holder looks like? Did you take any from Perry Austin's plate case after you had searched his desk?"

He felt the jolt of her answer before she spoke, because he saw that answer in the recoil of her eyes, the sudden deepening of the color in her throat. "Why—yes," she said weakly.

Casey took a long drink and sat down heavily. He put the glass aside and ran his fingers through his hair. He tried to keep his voice matter of fact. "Why?"

"When I found all those other pictures in the desk, when I realized what sort of person this man was—well, I noticed the plate case and opened it. I know something about cameras. I could tell some of the film holders were exposed and I—I just took them. I didn't know what they were but I didn't want the police to come and perhaps find another sordid picture like the one of my brother. I suppose it was some silly impulse but—"

"What did you do with them?"

"I still have them. I was going to develop them some time just to see—"

"Get them."

She turned and left the room. When she came back she had four film holders in her hand and a guilty look on her face.

Casey exhaled noisily. He couldn't be angry with her, nor was there any point in telling her that if she'd left them alone he could have developed them two days ago. He just bunched his lips and said, "When you search a guy's apartment you don't miss a thing, do you?"

"I'm sorry. It does sound rather silly now. Have I—made more trouble for you?"

"No," Casey said. "They probably don't amount to anything, anyway." And even as he spoke he thought, *This does it. If Dixon had killed Austin for the picture he would have searched that plate case. He didn't. He didn't even know he had it.* "I was just wor-ried about what happened to them," he said, and finished his drink quickly.

Nancy Jamison went to the door with him. "Do they know who killed him yet?"

"No."

"Will you come back again—if you find out anything more?"

Casey smiled down at her. "You've got paint on your nose," he said. "I'll probably come back whether I find out anything or not."

Her "don't forget," followed him down the stairs.

The afternoon city editions were on the street when Casey got back to the *Express*. He picked up a *News* and glanced at a two-column head with satisfaction. It said, *Police Seek Dixon, Arrest In Endicott Murder Near.*

He read on until he saw the sentence he was looking for: *According to the police, a new witness, thought to be a local news-paperman, has come forward with clear-cut evidence—* He folded the paper and went upstairs.

He tapped the four film holders in his coat pocket, answering Tom Wade's idle comments without knowing what he said, knowing that he could not develop the films here, that he must wait until he was home. As he got up to leave he told Wade he had an assignment and might not get back. He was at the door when the telephone rang. He waited for Wade to answer it.

"Just a minute," he said. "For you, Flash."

The voice that came to Casey was low and measured. "Casey? I've been reading the papers. Can you talk?"

Casey said to wait a minute, and motioned Wade from the room, cursing bluntly to make him hurry. "Okay," he said.

"Know who this is?" Casey said he could guess. "So you saw me, huh?" Dixon continued. "What were you waiting for?"

"The picture. I didn't find it until this morning."

"No?"

"I gave it to Austin that night in Endicott's office. He brought it over and put it in his desk. You didn't know about that, huh? Neither did I. I thought you copped it when you knocked him off, only it was in his desk. Tough, huh?"

"It's no good without you. It's only a picture. You have to be around to say where and when you got it. And you're not going to be around."

"Like Harry Nye?"

"And letting you know in advance."

"You scare me," Casey said. "I took care of your other two boys, I'll take care of any more you can find."

"I'm doing this personally," Dixon said. "This time it'll be me, Casey."

"Okay," said Casey. "It's a date."

CHAPTER TWENTY-ONE

WITH FROZEN NERVES

THE FOUR FILM HOLDERS that Perry Austin had taken home with him the night of his death yielded eight good negatives. Four of these Casey identified at once as the shots Austin had taken on assignment during the short time he was at the Club Berkely; the other four were of an entirely different nature.

All four of them were copies of some clippings or, papers, and in negative form Casey could not tell what they meant. The four of the girls at the Club he put aside, and as soon as the others were dry he adjusted the enlarger, took out some 11-by-14 paper and started to work, thinking about his plan and the arrangements Lieutenant Logan had made.

The plant would be about as foolproof as it could be made. Across the street, in the front room of a boarding-house, there would be a headquarters detective. He'd have a telephone at his elbow and a pair of night glasses within reach. There was no one hiding on the street. The street was open to Bernie Dixon whenever he wanted to come, and it was the same way in the back.

There was an alley behind the house Casey lived in and this alley was lighted at either end and also in the middle of the block, the back door of Casey's place being but 30 or 40 feet from this light. There was a fence behind the alley, a small back yard and an old apartment house. On the second floor rear would be another headquarters detective with telephone and glasses. Two blocks away Logan and Manahan would be waiting in a squad car.

Casey was satisfied. Bernie Dixon would not be scared off by running into anyone on the street. He could enter this house either by the front or back door, but not without being seen by one of the two detectives. The minute he entered, a phone call would warn Casey—an operator at the main office had been assigned to put the call through at once—and Casey would give headquarters a flash to be relayed by radio to Logan. Within two minutes of the time Dixon entered the house Logan, Manahan, and two plain-clothes men would be there. All that was needed now was a final call from Logan to tell him the trap was ready—

Casey felt the .38 special in his hip pocket and took the print out of the fixing bath. It showed an envelope, a legal-size envelope with Stanford Endicott's name in the upper lefthand corner. Across it was written *For Miss Lyda Hoyt*. That was all. Casey put it back in the fixing bath, stared at it; then something clicked inside his head and stirred his memory. The answer fell neatly into place.

"The envelope she went to Endicott's for," he said aloud and remembered what she had said in Logan's office, the commission she had given Endicott to get a pardon for her friend and how she had hurried there during intermission to get this envelope.

She never had a chance to get it because Casey had surprised her. But Perry Austin had the chance. There were eight or ten minutes while Casey was following Dixon when he could look over the offices. He had found this envelope and taken it, along with something else, something that pointed to Dixon as the killer.

What this something was, Casey did not know, or care. The envelope had nothing to do with Dixon or the murder and Austin had merely taken it because its contents looked promising. There would be a pardon inside, and Lyda Hoyt's name on the outside, and he had planned to sell that envelope for what he could get. The mistake he had made was in picking up something else in that office and then going to Dixon with it.

"The stupid fool!" Casey said bitterly. "He might just as well have cut his own throat as go to Dixon and try to shake him down. He knew by then he had killed Endicott."

The doorbell cut sharply across his thoughts, its shrill summons jarring his nerves. Startled into immobility he stood there for long seconds, feeling the tension wind up inside him. Dixon?

He waited, half expecting the telephone to ring. Then he remembered that he had not had the call from Logan yet, the one that was to tell him that all details had been arranged. Through the window he could see that it was already dark outside. And where the hell was Logan?

The bell rang again, stirring him to action. He pushed aside the darkroom curtain and went down the short hall to the living-room. Here he stopped, conscious of a strange tingling that vibrated all through him. He felt like a hunted animal waiting for the kill and realized this and that made him angry. "Nuts," he said softly and reached for the .38. He cocked it as he stepped to the door.

"Yes?"

"Western Union," a voice said.

Casey grunted to himself, "That's an old one." Aloud he said, "Shove it under the door."

"I can't. I got a package."

Casey turned the lock, drew back, bent an eye around the corner of the door. When he saw the uniform, he put the gun behind him and made the opening wider. He saw the small package in the boy's hand.

"Sign here."

Casey shoved the gun in his pocket, accepted the package and the receipt and pencil. "Wait a minute," he said, and shut the door.

He came back to the table, inspecting the package. He signed the paper, felt for a coin and found a quarter; then he went back, opened the door, and got rid of the boy. Back at the table he realized that the muscular stiffness that had crept over him had not yet released him. He laughed. An odd relief struck through him, and he jeered at himself.

"You're worse than an old woman. He chuckled again, realizing that it had not been fear as such, but uncertainty and suspense that had keyed him up. "Old lady Casey," he said and opened the package.

It proved to be an oblong leather box with the name of an exclusive jeweler imprinted on the cover. He lifted this and a card fell out which he caught in midair. Upon the velvet lining of the box was a wrist watch and when he saw it he sucked in his breath and blew it out in a soft whistle.

The name, *Mr. Grant Forrester,* was engraved on the card and there was some writing on the front and back. Casey read: *I hope this will replace the one I broke for you, and some day I want you to show me that right cross. It's a honey— Lyda sends her love— Grant.*

The glow that came over Casey was like that produced by 20-year-old brandy. He read the card over again and said, "A nice guy," and looked at the watch. It was thin, streamlined, and rectangular. It looked like platinum and he thought probably it was, and on the face was stamped *Patek-Philipe.* He strapped it on and was still admiring it when the telephone shrilled beside him. He jumped for it, pulse quickening again. "Yeah?"

It was Logan. His voice was calm, matter of fact. "Okay?" he said.

"Okay."

"We're all set. The sergeant and I'll be around until two or so and then somebody else'll be waiting. He may not show tonight but—take care of yourself now, you big ox."

Casey said he would and hung up. He put the card from Forrester in his pocket, glanced approvingly at the watch again, and went back to the darkroom.

When he saw the print of the envelope in the fixing bath, his thoughts came back to Lyda Hoyt—and Austin. He thought he knew what the other three negatives would yield. One would be a copy of the pardon Endicott had secured. The others? He held these two up to the safe-light. They looked like copies of newspaper clippings.

Ten minutes later he saw that he had been right. He did not bother to examine the three prints then, but left them in the fixing bath and started to clean up. Later, while the prints were washing, he made a drink and went back to the living-room. He sat with the drink and a cigarette for several minutes, thinking about many things until finally the focus was on Bernie Dixon. Down deep where he had buried it a single thought struggled for attention, and when it continued to nag him Casey got up and went to the bedroom.

From the night table, he took a small wooden-handled automatic. A Mauser. A .25 caliber and the lightest gun of its type he had ever owned. He balanced it in his palm, hefting it, his eyes narrowed in thought while one part of his brain insisted that he was being silly and the other argued just as strongly that he could afford to overlook no possibility, no matter how remote.

In the end, just a little sheepishly, he gave in to this second line of reasoning. A trap had been laid for Bernie Dixon. On the face of it, he did not seem to have a chance of getting in this apartment without being seen. Yet Dixon was a desperate man now, a hunted man. He had become convinced that Casey alone stood between him and a murder conviction. With Casey gone, Dixon could take his chances with the processes of law. He had money for the best lawyers and would be a hard man to convict; in fact he undoubtedly thought that he could *not* be convicted without Casey's testimony.

Well, that was okay. That was exactly what Casey wanted him to think. So—why take anything for granted? Why not take every available precaution? Just in case Dixon proved to be smarter than they expected him to be. *And don't forget either,* he thought, *Dixon's probably pretty clever with a gun, and you're not.*

"Hell, yes," Casey said. "I'm bait but no dope." He inspected the automatic, made sure there was a shell in the chamber, slipped on the safety. Over at the dresser, he rummaged in a drawer and found a man's sewing-kit someone had once given him. He had used it occasionally when important buttons came off, and now he found thread and tested the breaking strength of the four little spools.

The one he selected was black, and he sat on the bed, measured off a length, and made a noose at one end. He took off his coat and vest, slipped the noose over his head, and held the free end across his chest and down his right arm as far as the wrist, breaking off the thread at that point. After that he removed the noose, tied the other end to the trigger guard of the automatic.

He had some trouble getting his coat and vest on, and the gun adjusted the way he wanted it. He was afraid he might break the thread, and took it easy, stopping to curse himself for a fool now and then, but keeping at the job until, in the end, he stood up with the automatic hanging inside his coat sleeve, its muzzle about an inch back from the cuff. It felt all right and he didn't think it showed much of a bulge. He moved his arm this way and that, holding it out from his body and then shoulder high; finally he lowered it, deciding that unless someone was actually looking for a gun in his sleeve it would go unnoticed.

Back in the darkroom, he took the three remaining prints from the water, rolled them and put them on the drier. Then, keeping his curiosity in check until he could inspect them properly, he took all of them back to the living-room and sat down.

He put the photograph of the envelope on the floor and examined the one reproducing the pardon. He could read most of it and saw that it was signed by the governor of a Middle Western state and that it granted a full pardon to Lucille Miter for a conviction handed down 12 years previously. This, then, was the job Stanford Endicott had done for Lyda Hoyt, and repeating the name, Lucille Miter, half-aloud, Casey stared across the room, his frown putting funny humps and wrinkles in his face.

When his gaze finally came back to the photograph he dropped it beside the one of the envelope and inspected the remaining two, realizing that his guess about the negatives had been correct: both photographs were reproductions of newspaper clippings which looked old and discolored. The instant he read the first headline he knew why, for they were as old as the crime for which Lucille Miter was sentenced 12 years ago.

The first said, *Two Caught in Jewel Break,* and as Casey read the subhead and tried to follow the rest of the story he saw that it bore out the statement Lyda Hoyt had made. A man giving his name as Frank Sanger had tried to stick up a jewelry store, and the girl, who had been sitting outside in a car, was arrested as an accomplice.

The second clipping was smaller than the first and said,
Sentence Two in Holdup Attempt

Found guilty of the abortive attempt to hold up Steiger's jewelry store last month, Frank Sanger was sentenced by Judge Dunn this morning to serve five to ten years in the State Penitentiary. Lucille Miter, his pretty girl accomplice, was given a one-to-two year term in the Women's Reformatory. . . .

Casey thought, *It's all there. Except the clipping that tells about the accident and her escape.*

He was never sure how long he sat there thinking about these things he had read, and what Perry Austin had done. He smoked two cigarettes, hardly moving in his chair, holding the photographs in one hand but staring vacantly at the spot of blank wall over the divan. When the second cigarette burned his finger, he put it out and stood up.

Taking the prints back to the kitchen, he found the negatives, put them all together. In the lower drawer of his desk were some large-size envelopes and he folded the prints once and sealed them in the envelope, thinking all the time of Perry Austin. He walked back and forth across the room, his chin down and eyes morose, feeling now and then the pressure of the little automatic against his arm. When he noticed his empty glass he went back to the kitchen and made another drink. He had carried it back to the living-room when the doorbell rang loud and insistent.

The sudden explosion of sound stiffened Casey and he looked at the door, waiting for the ringing to stop. He put down the glass, and suddenly the tension was clamping about him. For the bell was still ringing, a jangling, discordant note that rolled on and on in nerve-fraying crescendo, piling up against his eardrums until he wanted to shout. When he could stand the sound no longer, he started for the door, reaching for his gun. He was about halfway there when the ringing stopped and the silence struck back. He had the gun in his hand now and had nearly opened the door before he remembered and called, "Who is it?"

"Got a message for you, Mister," a small voice said.

Casey could tell it was a child's voice, but it could still be a trick and he inched the door open carefully, the gun ready. Outside stood a small, dirty-nosed boy with an envelope in his hand.

"You Mr. Casey? Here." He thrust the envelope at Casey, wheeled and was gone.

"Hey. Wait a minute!" Casey said, but he could already hear the running feet on the stairs. "What the hell," he said, and put the gun away, and started to look at the envelope. He saw his name on the front of it, the apartment number. Then the telephone rang.

Still confused by the boy and his unexpected flight, he found the sudden clangor a startling, nerve-jarring sound and stared at the instrument as at something he had never before seen. A second ticked by. Then he remembered and jumped for it, a sudden apprehension vibrating along his spine. Was this it? Was there some connection between this ringing and the boy's note? He scooped at the telephone, stilled it.

The first thing he heard was a man swearing. Apparently not at him but at some operator, for the swearing broke off abruptly and the voice yelled, "Casey? He's on his way up. Back door—"

"Put it down! Now!"

The thin, taut voice coming from behind hit Casey like an avalanche. He caught his breath and stiffened, nerves frozen, every muscle tight. The back of his neck was all goose flesh. He could not move. He could not even think until the voice rapped at him again.

"Okay, then—"

Casey pushed the telephone away as though it had burned him, hearing another voice in the earpiece that sounded urgent but thin and indistinct. It stopped suddenly and he wondered about it until he realized he had hung up. He got his weight on both legs. It was a tremendous physical effort in those first few seconds to make himself move but he did, turning slowly, the bottom dropping out of his stomach.

Bernie Dixon was in the doorway of the inner hall. He had a heavy automatic in his hand. His coat collar was turned up and his hat brim was low; beneath it was a tight gray face and a hueless slash of a mouth.

CHAPTER TWENTY-TWO

NEAT AND QUICK

CASEY STOOD VERY STILL, some fragment of his brain sending out the curious thought that even now Dixon looked well-dressed and dapper. He was not exactly the Dixon of the Club Berkely, but he didn't have to be now. He moved slowly into the room with a sliding, flat-footed shuffle, his shrewd little eyes darting in all directions at once until he was satisfied they were alone. Only then did he relax and let his gaze become fixed.

"Turn around!"

Casey hesitated. He was still all tight and rigid inside, but he didn't want Dixon to know; he wanted to make him think there was all the time in the world.

"Hello, Bernie," he said, and glanced down at the envelope in his hand. "There isn't anything in this, is there? You sent the kid up to give the bell a good long ring so I wouldn't hear you unlock the back door, huh? Very neat."

Apparently Dixon didn't care for the digression. "I said, turn around!"

Casey took his turn deliberately.

"Hold your arms out!"

The gun hit him in the ribs as Dixon spoke and Casey put his elbows up, keeping his palms forward and bulging the muscles of his forearm against the little automatic in his sleeve. He felt Dixon's hand slap his hips and was curiously relieved, for this meant the man wasn't going to start shooting for a minute or so, not until he'd made his search.

The probing hand found the .38 special in Casey's hip pocket, withdrew it, continued patting his pockets and sides and armpits. When the pressure of the gun against his spine was removed, he turned.

Dixon had backed away; he was eyeing the gun he had taken from Casey, and the slash which was his mouth dipped at one corner. "I can use this one just as well," he said, and shifted it to his right hand. "Waiting for me, huh. Didn't think I could get in."

"You had a key," Casey said. "You couldn't have picked that lock while that bell was ringing."

"I came up the back way two days ago."

"After you found out your two hoods had fluffed it."

"Right. I didn't know what I was going to have to do and I like odds when I can get them. I made an impression of the lock and got a key. For a while I thought I wasn't going to have to use it— Who was that on the phone?"

"The office."

"You sure?" Dixon pushed back his hat with the muzzle of the automatic and Casey saw the film of moisture on the forehead.

"What difference does it make now?" he said.

"None, I guess. You asked for this and now you're gonna get it, Casey."

"And what happens to you?" Casey was keeping his voice level, now but all the time he was thinking, watching the narrow frames of Dixon's eyes, trying to read them, wondering how much time he had left. Where the hell was Logan? In another minute or two he ought to be outside with his men. But—how would they get in?

"Me?" Dixon grunted softly. "Nothing, maybe. Anyway, I have to take a chance, don't I? I might get away with this. I can hole up for a few months until I find out what the score is. What have I got to lose?"

Lamp light gleamed from Dixon's forehead now and made his skin look sallow. He was getting nervous and Casey knew it, knew that somehow he had to keep talking, keep Dixon's attention centered on what he said.

For Casey saw how the odds stood now. He had a gun up his sleeve but he couldn't hope to stand here and get it out and still have time to use it. The idea had seemed pretty cute at the time; now it didn't stand up so well. One bad move and Dixon would start shooting. That little automatic was no good unless he could shield his intention until he had it in his hand. Even then Dixon might beat him to the first shot.

"You'd've been all right, I guess," he said, "if it hadn't been for that bond rap against Endicott. He knew they had him cold and he was going to sing for a light sentence. And then the judge would've thrown the book at you." He went on, talking fast, never for an instant relaxing his study of the other's eyes. He told about Logan's theory, of the auto-accessory store and the wholesale jeweler who had served as outlets for stolen goods that Dixon and Endicott had provided.

"You know a lot," Dixon said.

"But you wouldn't leave Endicott's wife alone, would you? And so he put Harry Nye on you and got the goods. That made it sure Endicott would cop a plea if he could. Did you go down to his office to kill him or make up your mind after you got there?"

"Louise told me," Dixon said. "He'd popped off to her about getting even with me. I had an idea what he meant so I went down to make sure."

"And Nat Garrison nearly walked in on you."

"That was a break," Dixon said. "I ducked into the next room and held a gun on Endicott through a crack in the door until he got rid of the guy."

"And Harry Nye knew too much too, didn't he?" Casey asked.

Dixon's mouth screwed into a mean, hard line. "Nuts," he said. "What's all this stalling going to get you? Can you take it standing up?"

"What?" he said. "No music to cover up your blasting? I'm a little surprised at you, Bernie. This is an apartment house. You think you can turn it into a shooting gallery and walk out without being seen?"

He said other things, taunting things that had no particular meaning for him because he was trying desperately to find in which direction his best chance lay. For a moment he considered telling Dixon about Logan and the others, but he decided against that. Dixon had made his move. Like he said, he had nothing more to lose; if he suspected a trap he would shoot immediately.

No, that wasn't it. He had to get at the gun in his sleeve. He had to have noise so that Logan could get in the back way without being heard. He felt a quick thrust of hope when he saw the man's glance waver and stray to the radio cabinet, and was glad he'd thought to suggest it.

"Why not?" Dixon said. "You think of things." He gestured with Casey's .38. "Turn it on. Make it loud."

Casey's legs felt stiff and for the first step or two his feet seemed numb; then, suddenly, a change came over him. At first he did not understand it, but as he reached the radio he knew what had happened. Until this moment he had been too busy worrying about himself to remember that this was not the first time Dixon had hoped to kill him, and the thoughts of that other night came tumbling about him. The memory of that ride with Dixon's killers was stark and vivid. He'd felt fear that night, a cold and numbing fear that ate away his insides and bathed him in cold sweat. Now, remembering, thinking of this man who had been responsible, he found instead of fear and uncertainty, a quickly mounting resentment that became cold and calculating and vindictive.

What was he crabbing about? This was what he'd asked for, wasn't it? He hadn't expected things to turn out in just this way, but he'd offered himself as a decoy willingly and with eyes open—and for a special reason.

He had never before admitted the presence of this particular reason. This was the thought he had kept crowded deep in his consciousness, vaguely aware of it somehow but never quite daring to consider it properly. Now that there was nothing left with which to keep it in check, he found the thought clear cut and definite. It left him a little amazed, even now, when he realized that the focal point around which the idea revolved was the death of Bernie Dixon.

That morning, talking to Logan and MacGrath, he had suggested that Dixon might be trapped. Analyzing now, he knew why. Always in the back of his mind there had been that fear that Perry Austin's blackmailing would become known, and everything he had done had been motivated by the desire to keep all that a secret. And so, believing that any trial involving Dixon would bring to light Austin's career as an extortionist, he, Casey, had suggested a trap, a plant. And why? Because he hoped that Dixon, cornered, would resist arrest and be brought down by police guns and silenced forever.

"Well, what're you waiting for?"

The light in the cabinet went on and the dials glowed. "We have to wait a minute for it to warm up," he said and moved as naturally as he could to one side of the cabinet.

He was facing Dixon diagonally now, his right arm and part of his body blocked off from the other's sight by the cabinet. He forced his gaze back to the dials and with what looked like an absent gesture, reached inside his coat and began to scratch his shoulder. It was a bad second or two and the sweat began to leak down his back. But nothing happened and he found the thread along his arm and snapped it without stopping that pretense of scratching.

Gradually the radio came to life. Casey straightened, let his right hand straighten, feeling the nose of the automatic touch his palm and then easing it down until he could get hold of the little butt.

"Well, come on. Music, stupid."

Casey put on the grin again, not realizing until then that what he had was a quiz program. He turned the dial with his left hand, found a dance band.

"Louder," Dixon said.

Casey reached the volume control, turned it. The music swelled through the room, the rhythm pounding and the brasses riding high and loud. He saw Dixon's mouth set and the hand tighten on the gun, and thought, *This is it.*

All right, then. Things had changed since this morning, but one thing was still the same. Dixon on trial for murder would ruin everything Casey had tried to do. If Logan couldn't get here to do the job, then Casey had to do the best he could. Well— In a way this was what he wanted. He hadn't fired a gun in a long time but it was only ten or twelve feet and he could pull the trigger just as fast as Dixon.

"Okay," Dixon said. "Let's see if you can take it. Step out, Casey."

Casey looked into the muzzle of the .38. He was still thinking about the little .25 in his hand. That .38 was heavy and the first slug that hit him would slap him around some.

"All right, Bernie," he said and found he had to raise his voice against the music. "But this is a job you'll never walk out on." He started to move away from the cabinet and raise his gun hand, knowing he was going to pull the trigger twice and keep moving, dropping down if the first slug missed him and firing again from one knee. "The others didn't have a chance but this time—"

Casey was never quite sure what made him stop. He was watching Dixon and talking and tightening his trigger finger before he showed the gun, and then something happened he could not understand.

Dixon, standing near the center of the room, and in such a way that he could not see the hall doorway without turning his head, had leveled both guns. The right hand was already tensing as Casey moved out and then, incredulously, the hot, bright eyes wavered and darted to one side.

For some reason he could never explain Casey stopped, his gun up, the sharpest of sensations tearing along his nerves. The dance music was pounding his eardrums now, and hearing nothing but the hot, wild beat of the rhythm, with no warning but that quick flicker of alarm in Dixon's eyes, he waited, knowing that he could squeeze the trigger safely but obeying some intuitive command that stayed his finger.

Afterward he knew that Dixon had never seen that little automatic, that Dixon had heard some sound in the hall and, discounting Casey's presence, had turned to face it. For that was exactly what the man did, glancing over his shoulder first, never looking at his victim again, but wheeling toward a blur of movement in the doorway and a voice that yelled, "Drop 'em!"

Casey froze, his finger tight on the trigger but not quite tight enough, seeing Dixon try to get both guns around. He caught the gleam of Logan's service pistol, watched Dixon throw a quick, desperate shot before he was ready; then Logan's gun jumped and roared, and as the dance music faded into a softer chorus, Casey counted three shots so close together they were almost one.

Bernie Dixon stiffened with the first shot and the others seemed to make no difference. He began to fold in the middle as the echoes died away. The guns dropped from his hands; then he went down joint by joint, slowly, gracefully, with hardly a sound until he fell forward from his knees.

Logan walked into the room, his eyes on Dixon. Manahan and a plain-clothes man followed, guns hanging from their hands. They looked at Dixon and then up at Casey. Suddenly Manahan stopped. "Hey," he said. "Watch where you're pointing that." And not until then did Casey realize that he still had his arm out, the gun extended.

He looked at it curiously as he brought it over in front of him. He put it on the radio cabinet and looked at that a moment before he reached down and snapped off the current. His breath came out in a gust before he was aware that he had been holding it, and then reaction set in and he saw his hands were trembling.

"Where the hell were you?" he said, his voice an angry growl deep in his throat.

"Where was I?" Logan stared at him. "Where do you think? Out back. We didn't dare try to rush it. If it hadn't been for that radio—" He broke off, the scowl deepening. "Where'd you get that toy automatic?"

Casey interrupted to tell him about his plan of concealment.

"Well, I'll be damned," Logan said; then, angrily: "Why didn't you use it when he turned on me?"

Casey had an answer for this but he didn't state it. He'd wanted Logan with his authority to do it.

"When I saw you I forgot—or maybe I was scared."

"Yah!" jeered Logan. He pushed back his hat, walked around Dixon, picking up the fallen guns and putting them on the table. "What is this?" he asked, pointing to Casey's drink.

"That's mine," he said. "Give it to me. I need it."

He took it away from Logan and drank half of it, spilling a little on his chin. He saw a near-by chair and it looked awfully good to him. He sat down.

"How'd he get in?" Manahan asked.

Casey told him. "And what was your trouble?" he added when he finished. "You were supposed to have a guy call me—"

Logan began to curse and out of the profanity Casey got the explanation. The man watching the rear door had seen Dixon, but when he picked up the telephone the operator had delayed him just long enough to give Dixon his chance.

"A fine thing," Casey said. "I oughta sue the company."

Logan went to the telephone and began to rumble orders into it. Manahan looked at Casey's drink and pointedly licked his lips. "Any more of that?"

Casey sighed and got up. He went into the kitchen and got a bottle and glasses. Logan hung up and watched the sergeant and plain-clothes man pour drinks.

"Just one now," he said, "and then put that bottle away. It don't look good."

Casey emptied his glass and picked up the telephone.

"Who you calling?" Logan asked.

"The *Express*."

Logan opened his mouth as though to protest, thought better of it and closed it again. Casey asked for MacGrath and got him. "We got Dixon," he said. "Yeah. Right here in my apartment. . . . Dead. . . . Logan . . ." and for the next five minutes he answered the questions MacGrath asked. When he hung up he went to the entry-way closet and took out his plate case.

"Now wait a minute," Logan said irritably.

Casey gave him a long hard look.

"You know what the regulations are, Flash."

Casey kept looking and pulled out the camera.

"I ain't kiddin'."

"Neither am I," said Casey. "You got Dixon, didn't you?"

"Sure, but—"

"That cleans up three murders, don't it."

"Yeah, but—"

"And it's a lot better than trying to convict him in court, ain't it?"

"Sure, but—"

"You sound like Jack Benny," Casey said. "I'll answer my own questions. Did I help you? Yes. Could you have got Dixon without me?"

"We refuse to answer," Manahan said.

"I promised MacGrath some pictures," Casey said. "And he's going to get them. What do you think of that?"

Logan checked his reply and watched Casey open a tripod. He glanced over at Manahan and shrugged.

CHAPTER TWENTY-THREE

AMONG FRIENDS

THERE WAS A CRACK OF LIGHT showing under the door and Casey knocked, and that started a wheezing and grunting that was loud enough to filter though the panel. A chair creaked and presently the floorboards took up the sound and he glanced down, half-expecting to feel the actual vibration. He did not hear the Capehart, so low was it turned, until Jim Bishop opened the door.

"Hello, Jim."

Bishop just stared at him for a moment, hanging onto the door-knob, the other arm propped against the jamb. He was wearing slippers and a shirt open at the throat. His fat face looked puzzled. "Well," he said finally, "Casey."

"I was coming by," Casey said. "I thought I'd see if you were up."

"Come in." Bishop walked away from the door and lowered himself laboriously into the chair, sighing loudly when he made it. Casey closed the door and tossed his hat onto the table. He unbuttoned his balmacaan and fanned it out as he sat down.

"I just finished up a three-hour session with Logan. They got Bernie Dixon tonight. I thought you'd like to know."

A second or two ticked by before Bishop replied. He slid his hands along the chair arms, his eyes intent but lost in shadow. "They did, huh?" he said at last. "Alive?"

"Logan got him," Casey said, and went on to explain what had happened at his apartment and how Dixon had died.

Bishop listened without interruption, nothing moving in his face. Finally he said, the old familiar hoarseness in his voice, "You took an awful chance, didn't you? You knew Dixon would gun you out if he could. Why should you do a thing like that?"

"I had a reason." Casey took a folded envelope from his coat pocket and balanced it on his knee. "It all goes back to Perry Austin. He was a blackmailer, Jim. He and Harry Nye were shaking down people all over town. I couldn't let anybody find out about it." He looked down at the envelope, picked it up. "This is something you'll probably want."

Bishop sat up and took the envelope, not looking at it but watching Casey and opening it by touch. He took out four photographs but it seemed to require quite an effort on his part to pull his gaze from Casey and look at them.

"Where did you get these, Flash?"

"I have to go back a couple of days," Casey, said. "That morning when we were in Logan's office, he wanted to know why your niece went to see Endicott in the first place, and she told him about this friend of hers who had been in a jam years ago. She said this friend was married now and going to have a baby. She said this friend was afraid of an old sentence hanging over her and that she—your niece—had gone to Endicott to see if he could get a pardon and close the case."

"Oh," Bishop said, his voice curiously soft.

"But Lyda Hoyt didn't get that envelope that night Endicott was killed because I scared her off. And it couldn't have been there, anyway, because Austin had already picked it up—while I was out chasing Dixon. He took it back to the *Express* and made these copies. The trouble is, the film holders got lost—I don't have to tell you how—and I didn't get ahold of them until today. When I developed them this afternoon I thought you'd want them."

"God, yes." Bishop tucked the photographs and negatives back into the envelope with fat, trembling hands. "These could make a lot of trouble for that girl."

Casey reached for a cigarette. He tapped it thoroughly, rolled it gently between thumb and fingers, and pulled a flake of tobacco from one end. "Is that all, Jim?" he asked, not looking up.

"All?"

"Don't you care about the original envelope? The one Austin photographed?"

"Why—why, yes," Bishop stammered. "Of course, but—"

Casey looked up, seeing the shiny, twisted face, the silent working of the lips. He spoke quietly. "No, Jim. You're not worrying about the original. What did you do with it? Burn it?" He waited a moment. Bishop's eyes came into sharp focus and his mouth grew keen and hard. "And the key, Jim. You brought that away with you, didn't you?"

"The key?"

"Yes. To Austin's apartment." Casey stood up. He walked across the room and came back, stealing a glance at Bishop and finding the heavy face set and impassive, the eyes watching every move he made. The reply was a while in coming, but in the end it came on the heels of a flat and scornful laugh.

"By God, you are serious, aren't you? Maybe you'd better let me in on it."

"It's going to take a while."

"All right." The chair creaked and Bishop hoisted himself erect. "Then I'd better get me a beer," he said. "You?"

Casey said he guessed not and watched Bishop waddle through a doorway. He walked over to the chessboard that was laid out as it had been the other night, and picked up one of the figures. He took it with him to his chair and sat down, waiting until Bishop returned with his beer and settled himself.

"There were things that should have made me think of you a long time ago, Jim," Casey said. "Little things, but I guess a good detective would have been able to use them. Only I'm just a dumb camera. Until Austin was found I didn't care much about the murder of Endicott one way or the other. I thought I might have a picture of the killer but I didn't think it would be good enough to count, and I couldn't find it anyway. I had a picture of Lydia Hoyt, too, but that only complicated things and made more grief for me. But when I found Austin I jumped to conclusions because I thought he'd been killed for the picture I took of the killer in the sedan."

He went on to explain what had happened to the film holder, and how Finell had kept it in his coat pocket. "Then, a little later," he said, "I got the dope on Austin. I got some films—how I got them doesn't matter—that proved Austin had been blackmailing ever since he'd been in town. Not big stuff, but he'd apparently hooked up with Harry Nye, and they did some framing and made quite a thing out of it." He spread his hands. "But even then I figured Dixon had killed him. I figured he'd got some dope on Dixon from Endicott's office and tried to collect. When Harry Nye was found that was all right too, because Logan had a sound theory about Endicott and Dixon and Nye."

He explained this theory, told of the stolen-property racket that had made so much money for Endicott, and how Endicott, finding out about Dixon and his wife, had apparently decided to turn State's evidence and send Dixon to prison.

"Endicott was caught on the bond charge," he said, "and he could help himself and make it worse for Dixon by singing. That's why he was killed. And Nye was the last link with Endicott and the racket and he had to go too. He may even have known that Dixon murdered Endicott. Anyway, it all fitted in and Logan accepted my motive for Austin's murder—that he had been killed because Dixon thought he had the photograph I took."

Casey took a deep breath and grunted softly. "Not until I began to see your motive and suspect you, did I think of things I should have remembered before. First, you had the opportunity. Austin was killed between twelve and twelve-thirty. You left my office that first night in plenty of time. You went directly there, didn't you?"

Bishop sipped beer and said nothing.

"The next morning," Casey said, "two empty shells were found by Austin's body. I stepped on one and bent it out of shape. I didn't tell Logan that when he showed the two of them to me because the other shell was bent *practically flat*. I weigh two-fifteen, Jim, but I didn't bend my shell flat. You must weigh two-seventy—"

"Eighty," Bishop added.

"—and when you step on something you really flatten it. There it was if a guy could see it. Nothing conclusive, you understand, but just a suggestion that maybe the reason one shell was flat was because a heavier guy than I had stepped on it. So I muffed it. And I muffed something else. So did Logan, but he didn't have all the facts and I did."

Casey thought a moment and continued. "Bernie Dixon could not possibly have killed Perry Austin. Because from twelve to twelve-thirty that night Dixon was on the air, acting as a master of ceremonies at that model contest he was running. I knew that. So did Logan, I think. With me it meant nothing because when Dixon mentioned that, I didn't know *when* Austin had died, I didn't know until a day or two later. I didn't even remember it until late this afternoon. With Logan—if he knew about Dixon—there was an excuse because he could think the two hoods Dixon hired to put me away could have done the job. But me—I knew better."

His laugh came harsh and abrupt. "This'll give you an idea of why I'm a camera and not a detective. Those two hoods could not have killed Austin because at the time he died they were up searching my desk and the studio and slugging Finell. Not all that time, maybe, but they must have been there awhile before Finell arrived, and that was at twelve-fifteen. They couldn't have been two places at once, but Casey couldn't figure that one out. Casey was too busy worrying about what Austin had been doing, too busy trying to cover up." He paused, scowling. "And I'm glad I did," he said. "Not till this afternoon when I began to think about you could I see the facts."

Bishop put his beer glass aside. "You haven't told me yet why you should be figuring it was me."

Casey opened his hand, disclosing the chessman he had been holding. "What's this, Jim?"

Bishop looked at it quite a while. Finally he sighed ponderously. "A bishop," he said.

"What's the shape of the head?"

"Miter-shaped, like a bishop is."

Casey tossed it in the fat man's lap. "Now you know," he said. "When I read the pardon and saw those clippings, I knew. Lucille Miter, the girl's name was—the one that was sentenced." He paused. When Bishop remained silent, he continued. "Did you ever notice how people almost always use the same initials or a name that is similar in some way to their own name when they pick an alias? *Lucille Miter—Lucille Bishop*. She played chess, even as a kid, didn't she, Jim? She got pinched and wouldn't give her right name. The Lyda Hoyt came later. She isn't your niece, Jim, she's your daughter."

Bishop just looked at him, nothing changing in his face, his eyes still in shadow. Casey waited and the silence began to pile up. After what seemed like a long, long time, Bishop stirred. "A hunch, Flash," he said. "That's all you've got."

"No," Casey said. "I haven't finished. The guy Lucille Miter ran away with—she did run away, didn't she?—was named Frank Sanger according to those clippings. *The man you killed in the back room of a saloon a few years ago, in what was supposed to be a drunken brawl, was Frank Sanger.* The night you came to see me I remembered the case but I couldn't think of the name. I thought it was Sanford or Sanburn or something like that. It was Sanger, Jim. I remembered when I saw it in black and white."

Jim Bishop derricked himself slowly from the chair. He produced a handkerchief and mopped his pale, moist face. He put the chessman on the board and went to the desk and opened a drawer. When he turned he had a piece of paper in his hand—and a gun.

Casey sat very still, feeling the blood drain from his face and a slackness come over it. There might have been a moment, at the very first, when he could have jumped for that gun, but he had not figured on this and surprise robbed him of that moment, and now it was too late. He knew Bishop was moving back to the chair but he did not see him; all he saw was the gun.

CHAPTER TWENTY-FOUR

ONLY THE DEAD ARE SILENT

JIM BISHOP SAT DOWN HEAVILY, watching Casey with half hidden, inscrutable eyes. He leaned back and put the paper on the chair arm and the gun on top of it, within easy reach of his hand.

Casey wet his lips, swallowed, and spoke in measured tones. "I guess I didn't get my idea across very well."

"What idea?"

"Of why I bothered to come here."

"I don't know." Bishop rubbed his palms gently up and down the chair arms. "I don't know, Flash. But you've done a lot of talking and I guess it should be my turn. You want to take your coat off?"

"I'm okay," Casey said, wondering how the man could be so matter-of-fact.

Bishop nodded. "You think Logan's satisfied?"

"About Dixon? Sure he is. According to the story the D.A. gave out to the papers, that case is closed and everybody's damned glad it is because it looked tough."

"Then nobody knows about it—this other, I mean—but you and me? Well, I'd say you did all right. You talk about overlooking clues here and there but that's a lot of hooey. You're pretty close to tops, Flash. You always were. And you're right about Lyda. She's my daughter and her name was Lucille Bishop like you figured."

He glanced down at the gun and back again. "The story I gave you the other night was pretty close, all except the niece part. Lucille's—Lyda's—mother died when she was ten and I put her in a convent. I was in New York then and always a bit of a boozer and her mother's death hit me pretty hard and that didn't help any, but I wanted to be sure Lyda was brought up right. Well, when she was seventeen she left the school and came to live with me.

"I got a housekeeper—she wasn't worth a damn—and working nights like I was, I wanted to be sure Lyda didn't get chasing around. So I was too strict. I clamped down. I didn't understand that she was growing up and needed some freedom and boy friends. I guess some parents have always made that mistake, and anyway, I did. The details aren't important, but what happened was that she met Frank Sanger at some dance hall, and I found out and laid down the law and locked her up and a week later when I thought it had all blown over, she ran away with him."

He let his chins rest on his chest and watched Casey through his brows. "The rest of it is like I told you before. I never saw her again until she looked me up a few years ago. That's what made a tramp of me, realizing it was my fault. That's why I got canned in New York and why I came up here doing police reporting for a third of my old salary. I didn't know where Lyda was. I guess I thought she was dead. I'd even seen pictures of Lyda Hoyt, mind you, without recognizing her. Because at eighteen she was plump and rounded and full-faced and—well, you know how Lyda is. I just never saw any resemblance until that night she came to my apartment and told me who she was and how she'd had me traced."

"That's when you found out about the reformatory business," Casey said.

"Sure. She told me everything. How they'd driven West—she and Sanger—and how a couple of days later in Ohio this rat had tried to stick up the jewelry store. She didn't know what it was all about but she made up her mind I wasn't going to know what had happened. You can guess how a kid like that, running away, would take it. And she thought of the name, Miter, and used it. And then on her way to the reformatory the car crashed. The deputy that had her broke an ankle and she saw he wasn't hurt much and ran."

He hesitated, grunting softly. "Well, things like that happen, I guess. You wouldn't think she'd have a chance, but she had voice training and that helped—she was a waitress first until she got a job singing in a speak-easy—and damned if she didn't go from there to a girl act that was sent over to France. Then England—and you know the rest. All except about Sanger."

"He knew who she was," Casey said.

"The only one that recognized Lyda Hoyt and knew the truth. He'd been out of prison a few months when he found me. He wanted enough money to take him to England. That's where Lyda was then. He said either that or he'd blow the lid off proper."

All at once Bishop's fatty face was hard and his stare was flinty. "Can you imagine me letting him bleed her? It was my fault that she ran away. Everything was my fault. In spite of that, look what she'd made of herself—and alone too. Let a rat like Sanger ruin her life? No. Nor would you. I told him I'd get some money. I made a date in that bar and went early to get a little drunk and acted drunker than I was. The rest was easy. A quarrel that nobody could figure out, with me egging him on so it looked as though it was mostly his fault."

Casey let his breath out slowly and decided he didn't want to think about it any more. "I never figured you as that clever, Jim," he said.

"A man can be clever when he has to."

"You took an awful chance. Suppose Lyda had found out—or did she?"

"She didn't," Bishop said. "Of course I took a chance, but I had the odds with me. She was in England and the show looked good for a long time. I knew Sanger had a record and that it would come out. I pleaded guilty to manslaughter with no argument. Hell, the story never even made page three. Just another sordid barroom brawl, played down by the papers because I was one of the boys. I knew it would be that way. I got a letter to Lyda and said I was serving time and if she tried to get in touch with me I'd commit suicide. By the time she got back from England I was practically ready for parole. She never even asked me how it happened. She's that kind of a woman. That's why I had to take my chance with Austin."

He went on deliberately. "She was going to marry Forrester but she wouldn't do it unless she got that pardon—just like the story she told you. I argued for days but it was no good. She was going to do it her way. I sent her to Endicott and gave her the story to tell him—about this Lucille Miter being her friend. I didn't know he was a crook. I thought he was the best in town. At that he did a good job. And then he gets killed and Austin finds the envelope and, not knowing the truth probably, but figuring it's worth dough, calls her up."

"I thought it must have been something like that," Casey said. "She called you and told you Austin had the envelope and I had a picture of her. What a spot."

"'I told her I thought I could get the picture back because you were a regular," Bishop said.

"And what did you tell her about Austin? You knew you were going to kill him then, didn't you?"

"I think I did. Only the dead are silent, Flash, and I couldn't take a chance with Austin or any other man with blackmail in his mind, not with Lyda in love, not after I'd killed Sanger. Again it was my fault—I'd sent her to Endicott—but the tough part was how to do the job and not have her catch on— Well, Endicott had given her a flat price for his work. Five thousand if he was successful. So she had the money. I told her to make a date with Austin at his apartment for twelve-thirty and go there and buy back the envelope."

"She went there that night?"

"Sure. I knew she wouldn't be able to get in, because I got there at twelve. He tried to get a gun out when he saw what I was up to and I got it away from him and used it."

"You damn near missed," Casey said. "I was there at twelve-fifteen." And although he did not say so he thought, *And Nancy Jamison was there five minutes before that.*

The knowledge left him strangely shaken until Bishop said, "I was out of there by five after twelve or so and locked the door. It didn't take long." He paused and when he continued his voice was low and savage. "I didn't know he'd taken pictures of those papers."

His eyes focused again on Casey. The silence between them began to pile up and for the first time Casey really heard the muted Capehart. It was playing something from Sibelius, a somber, heavy piece that seemed to furnish just the right background, winding the tension inside him tighter and tighter. He tried not to look at the gun, but he couldn't help it and then, as he watched, he saw a puffy hand reach over and pick it up.

Something cold tripped up his spine and the skin at the back of his neck began to prickle. He pried his gaze from the gun. Bishop was still watching him. His lids were, narrow and behind them the eyes seemed fixed and inscrutable. Slowly he shifted the gun and began to lean forward. Casey started to speak and found he had to clear his throat first, it was so dry. He swallowed. He heard his voice as though he was speaking a yard away. "What're you going to do with that?"

For a moment Bishop stared at him, finally glancing at the gun, but only for an instant. His face twisted. He squinted so that his eyes were all but lost in the folds of surrounding flesh. He sat that way for interminable seconds before he moved and then, gradually, his lids opened and Casey could see his eyes again as he leaned back, lowering the gun.

"Why, you crazy damn fool!" he said with hoarse incredulity. "Did—did you think I was going to use it on you?"

The tight bands around Casey's chest that had been clamped there by his thoughts fell apart and his relief was overwhelming. Only then did he realize what had happened to him; only then did he realize that from the moment he had seen the gun his imagination had been slowly building up a distorted conclusion, an unwarranted vision of fear and dismay made vivid not so much by the situation as by nerves already frayed and ragged. Now the sweat of reaction was on his face and a muscular weakness came over him. "I didn't know," he said thickly, "the way you took it out."

"For God's sake, why? Do you think I go around killing guys because I like to? You could have told Forrester about me, you could have gummed things up any time you wanted to."

"You and I are still the only ones that know the truth. You said only the dead are silent."

"Sure," Bishop said. "But it doesn't change anything. No. That's not why I got the gun. I just wanted to show you what I had in mind. I couldn't tell you at first because I didn't know how much you knew."

As he spoke he picked up the paper under the gun and gave it to Casey. It was an unfinished letter addressed to MacGrath at the *Express* and said, *This is the best way for me when those heart attacks come, and a bullet is a lot easier. This check will pay for the undertaker and the bills, and as a last request, keep the obit down to a sticky.*

Casey handed back the note and stood up. "There's a reason for that now, maybe," he said, "but what was the reason before you knew I had the answer?"

"I guess I was scared," Bishop said. "I was afraid that when the police got Dixon and he got talking they'd find out he wasn't guilty of the Austin job. And then they would have started again and that Logan is the kind of a guy I wouldn't want on my neck. I didn't want to take any chances. You know I didn't kid you about my ticker, I'm likely to go off any day, Flash. So why take chances with Logan?"

"What about your daughter?"

"That's why I waited until tonight. She's gone to Hollywood. I was going to write her. She'd believe me if I sent a letter out—I'd be buried by the time she got it—saying I had another attack and couldn't stand the pain. She'd believe that, Flash. And so would the police. I was going to leave a note for them too. They'd check with my doctor and believe it. Simple enough, isn't it?"

"I guess so," Casey said, and suddenly he felt very tired and depressed and old. He felt lousy. There wasn't much left for him to say.

"I was writing that one when you knocked," Bishop said. "I'll finish the others after you leave. You don't mind giving me a little time, do you?"

Jim Bishop asked that favor simply, earnestly, and somewhere in Casey's neck a cord tightened. He looked down at the floor, scuffed it with his toe.

"You don't have to do this on my account, you know," he said.

"But—" Bishop sounded surprised and Casey answered him.

"I guess you still haven't got it straight just why I came," he said. "For the past couple of days I've done more covering up for Austin than I've ever done before in my life. I couldn't let that rotten business come out if I could help it. I was ashamed of him, and all the other cameras in town would be ashamed when they knew. I wanted to trap Dixon because I hoped Logan would shoot him down and keep him from talking. When I found out it was you, I had the same idea you just told me. If Dixon was caught, Logan would eventually find you were his man. So I still wanted Dixon shot. I would have done it myself."

He grunted bitterly. "Of course, he was going to kill me too, so technically that made a difference and gave me a right to shoot. It didn't come out that way, but I'm telling you what I had in mind. My hands aren't exactly clean either, but I don't think I'll lose any sleep over it. Dixon's better off dead. He got what was coming to him. And you—"

He broke off, tried again. "Well, if I'd wanted to turn you in I could have told Logan the same things I told you. I didn't. Not because I liked you, or ever figured you were justified. That didn't enter into it one way or the other. The point was, the law was satisfied and I knew I'd rather let you get away with it—for as long as your heart held out—than let all those things I'd covered up for Austin come to light again. I just stopped by to tell you how it was, to let you know you didn't quite get away with it."

"So that's how it is," he said. "I never should have got mixed up in the lousy case in the first place, but maybe I'm glad at that. This other—well, you don't have to do it on my account, but neither do I think I should try to argue you out of using the gun if that's what you want. You had a job to do, and you did it damn well, and now you have to figure the rest of it out yourself. Me, I've meddled enough. I'm washed up, finished with it, done."

"I believe you," Bishop said. "And thanks."

"For what?"

"For putting it just that way." Bishop had a crooked smile on his lips now and in his eyes there was a curious softness, a gentleness that seemed very young and did not go with his face. He watched Casey clap on his hat and said, "You understand things, Flash. You know I've got no regrets, that if I had to do it all over, I'd have a crack at it."

"I guess you would," Casey said, and went into the hall.

Bishop followed him. "What happens now doesn't matter," he said. "Only—either way I guess we won't be seeing each other any more. And if you don't mind too much, I'd like to shake hands before you go."

Casey looked down at the hand and took it, feeling the hot, hard pressure of it. He didn't look up again. He started to say something but his throat was tight then, so he turned quickly and went along the hall, hearing the door close softly as he started down the stairs.

The night air felt cool and fresh against his hot face and he tried to project his thoughts a million miles away. But it was no good. He knew it wouldn't work. He wanted to go see Nancy Jamison, not to talk but just to sit awhile, for there was a desperate loneliness moving with him that he could not cast aside. But it was too late for that now, and so, because he did not want to fight the torment any more, he knew he might as well go home and get a little drunk, and go to bed, being sure to put his felt silencer in the telephone so that if a call should come about Jim Bishop he would not know of it until morning.

MYSTERIOUSPRESS.COM

Otto Penzler, owner of the Mysterious Bookshop in Manhattan, founded the Mysterious Press in 1975. Penzler quickly became known for his outstanding selection of mystery, crime, and suspense books, both from his imprint and in his store. The imprint was devoted to printing the best books in these genres, using fine paper and top dust-jacket artists, as well as offering many limited, signed editions.

Now the Mysterious Press has gone digital, publishing ebooks through **MysteriousPress.com**.

MysteriousPress.com offers readers essential noir and suspense fiction, hard-boiled crime novels, and the latest thrillers from both debut authors and mystery masters. Discover classics and new voices, all from one legendary source.

FIND OUT MORE AT

WWW.MYSTERIOUSPRESS.COM

FOLLOW US:

@emysteries and Facebook.com/MysteriousPressCom

MysteriousPress.com is one of a select group of publishing partners of Open Road Integrated Media, Inc.

OPEN ROAD
INTEGRATED MEDIA

Open Road Integrated Media is a digital publisher and multimedia content company. Open Road creates connections between authors and their audiences by marketing its ebooks through a new proprietary online platform, which uses premium video content and social media.

Videos, Archival Documents, and New Releases

Sign up for the Open Road Media newsletter and get news delivered straight to your inbox.

Sign up now at
www.openroadmedia.com/newsletters